11 Paper Hearts

11 Paper Hearts

Kelsey Hartwell

Underlined

GetUnderlined.com

Educators and librarians, for a variety of teaching tools, visit us at RHTeachersLibrarians.com

Library of Congress Cataloging-in-Publication Data
Names: Hartwell, Kelsey, author.
Title: 11 paper hearts / Kelsey Hartwell. Other titles: Eleven paper hearts
Description: New York : Underlined, [2021] | Audience: Ages 12 and up. | Summary: A year after a car accident affected her memory, sixteen-year-old Ella begins receiving paper hearts from a secret admirer with clues that may help her remember the weeks she lost.
Identifiers: LCCN 2020029758 (print) | LCCN 2020029759 (ebook) |
ISBN 978-0-593-18007-5 (trade paperback) | ISBN 978-0-593-18008-2 (ebook)
Subjects: CYAC: Memory—Fiction. | Traffic accidents—Fiction. | Love—Fiction. |
Friendship—Fiction. | Valentine's Day—Fiction.
Classification: LCC PZ7.1.H3768 Aah 2021 (print) | LCC PZ7.1.H3768 (ebook) |
DDC [Fic]—dc23

The text of this book is set in 11-point Warnock Pro Lt.
Interior design by Cathy Bobak

Printed in the United States of America
10 9 8 7 6 5 4 3 2 1
First Edition

To my mom, my dad, my brother, and Belle

Prologue

I DON'T KEEP MANY SECRETS, BUT THE ONES I DO HAVE ARE hidden underneath a loose floorboard next to my bed.

There are over-the-top diary entries and poems about my deepest crushes—the ones only Carmen knew about. A valentine Adam Gurner gave me in the third grade that I've looked at so many times, I could practically forge his signature. A wrapper from the field trip where Adam offered me a piece of gum. When I got to high school, my secret stash became a little more interesting. There's a birthday card from my first and only boyfriend for my sixteenth birthday signed *Love, Pete*. Every time I look at it, I remember how Carmen squealed because that was the closest thing either of us had heard to *I love you*.

These are just a few of the mementos I keep in my secret

hiding place. No one even knows about the loose floor-board in my room, including my parents, because I hide it under a big fuzzy rug. Whenever I look inside the pocket in my floor, it's a little bit like looking inside my heart. Each item by itself may seem insignificant—but that's the point.

You see, I believe that everyone gets a love story—but you never know when it's going to happen. Like maybe you'll randomly bump into someone at a concert when the band is playing your favorite song. Or maybe you'll lock eyes with some cute stranger across a crowded room. I'm not sure about love at first sight—my mom says true love takes time. But what I do imagine is that you can look back to the moment you met someone you love and think, *yeah, I should've known then.* Because all of your favorite things about them were true then too, staring at you right in the face . . . and you remember how your heart was beating out of your chest. So you decide that it *was* love—the beginning of it—and you just didn't know that yet. Sometimes I think I keep things as simple as a gum wrapper in case these small moments are just the start of something real. Then I can look back and remember everything.

That's what I thought anyways . . . until I had no recollection. There are three things stashed in my hiding place that I don't remember saving:

1. A dried rose
2. A Polaroid of me next to a lamppost, looking at the photographer with the biggest smile I've ever seen on my face.
3. A bronze key

When I look at these three things, I think maybe I do have more secrets than I thought—even from myself.

Last year I was in an accident coming home from the Valentine's Day Dance at school. It was late at night and snowing the kind of snow that sticks immediately but not bad enough that people say to stay off the streets. I slid off the road on black ice into a tree. But I don't remember this. All I know is what my friends and family have told me and the details that pop up when you google Ella Fitzpatrick.

When I used to search my name to see what college admissions might find, only articles of me volunteering would appear. Now the first thing that comes up in the search engine before I even finish typing is *Ella Fitzpatrick accident.*

I cringe every time.

Because the thing is, when people see the articles, they must see a tragedy. But it wasn't. Not really.

Whenever I feel sorry for myself, I remember I'm lucky for so many reasons. This isn't one of those stories where there was a drunk driver involved or someone with me in the passenger seat died; I'm lucky that Carmen was able to raise money on a GoFundMe account so my family could pay the overwhelming medical bills. Most of all, I'm lucky that my brain bleed stopped when it did.

I even consider myself incredibly lucky for the little things. I'm lucky that I was sixteen and a minor so my picture wasn't plastered on the news. I'm lucky that the accident happened in February, and after my recovery six months later, I was able to make up missed work during summer school so I didn't fall behind. I'm lucky that when I asked to see Pete at the hospital, he came without question even though I had broken up with him three weeks before the accident.

Why couldn't I remember breaking up with him? Well, there were a lot of things I couldn't remember after the accident, like those three items I stored underneath the floorboard.

But I'm also lucky when it comes to my memory loss. Doctors have told me that amnesia is really rare, but when it happens people lose large amounts of time. *Years.* But I only lost a mere two and a half months. Seventy-seven days. Eleven short weeks of my life.

Still, I want to remember. Only whenever I think back to Valentine's Day, my brain feels like it has been bitten into like the end of a lollipop.

But this isn't a tragic story about the eleven weeks I lost.

It's about the eleven paper hearts I discover a year later.

Chapter 1

IT'S THE FIRST FRIDAY OF FEBRUARY AND I KNOW THREE things.

One, Valentine's Day decorations are already up all over school. Red and pink streamers are hung from the ceilings every year to make it feel like love really is in the air. But to me, it screams that love can be torn down at any second.

Two, I miss the days when teachers made everyone from the weird kid that picks his nose in the back of the classroom to your first Top-Secret Crush buy you a valentine. Even though their moms would just buy a pack of generic cards from Target and scribble their names at the bottom, it was something. Now that I don't have a boyfriend, who knows what I'll be getting.

Three, I know my new animosity for Valentine's Day really has nothing to do with these things and everything to do with what happened this time last year.

But I brush that thought aside harder than I brushed the knots out of my hair this morning to make it perfectly straight. Today I'm wearing a printed skirt with a cropped sweater and matching tights. I try to look my best even when I'm not feeling it, which is probably why my friends never know when something is bothering me.

We're huddled together in line for the paper hearts the student government is selling as a fund-raiser for the Valentine's Day Dance. There's a table set up outside the gymnasium, which is the perfect spot because it's where people always hang out before homeroom. A long line has formed from the gym entrance to the boys' locker room around the corner.

There's a part of me that's super proud of the turnout. The paper hearts were my idea in ninth grade when I first joined student government's planning committee. We were trying to think of something original to sell other than carnations to raise money for the Valentine's Day Dance. I thought of love letters immediately. There's something about them that feels so perfectly nostalgic. From there, I thought of selling paper cutouts in the shape of hearts people could write messages on, which would then be passed out around school during the weeks leading up to the dance. You can decorate them and write anything you want to. People mainly send short but sweet ones to their friends. Other times if you're in a relationship you might send a more thoughtful one to show how much you care. What's more romantic than telling someone how you feel?

Ever since freshman year I've gotten a heart from Pete. He isn't the sentimental type, but he always took them seriously. Part of me thinks it's only because it was my idea. But there's another part of me that feels it was genuine—he knew it made me really happy to open one from him.

There's something about receiving love letters that feels way better than some text. I saved all of them in the secret hiding spot next to my bed.

Standing in line, I wonder if any of the paper hearts I get this year will be worth keeping.

"We should get ours for free," Carmen declares as we inch toward the student government table. "Since this was Ella's idea."

Jessica and Katie nod. I glance up at the girl passing out the paper hearts. I forget her name somehow, even though she's the one who always raises her hand in my English class to answer all the questions. I don't really know her personally, but she doesn't exactly scream *rule breaker*.

I shake my head. "Not going to happen. But on the positive side, the money goes toward the dance."

"Oooh. Do you think there's going to be a flower wall for pictures again?" Katie asks.

I blink at the word *again*. I don't remember the flower wall.

Carmen gives Katie a look before answering. "Doubtful. Ella was the only one in student government who actually did anything cool. At least they're doing the paper hearts again instead of passing out dinky carnations. I wouldn't put that past them."

I force a smile like I do a lot lately. I used to *love* being on the planning committee, especially when it came to school dances. One of my favorite things has always been bringing friends together. In middle school, I started organizing big sleepovers complete with games, karaoke sing-offs, and Sephora face masks. They got so popular that my mom had to make me put a cap on who could come. By high school, I graduated to bigger events like school dances as the student body's social chair. But this year I just couldn't bring myself to do it.

"How many hearts do you think I'll get this time?" Jessica asks. "Last year I only got fourteen."

Katie rolls her eyes. "*Only* fourteen? Humble brag a little more, will you."

"Oh, save it," Carmen says. "Besides, paper hearts are about quality over quantity," she says before lightly elbowing me. "Who do you want to get one from?"

I shrug. "I don't even know who I'm sending one to besides you three and Ashley. But she's too cool for school these days. I bet she doesn't even send me one back."

"Forget your sister. What about Pete?" She winks.

I raise my eyebrow. The last person I expect a heart from is my ex-boyfriend, but no matter how many times I insist we're over, she brings him up whenever she can.

"Fine," she says, crossing her arms. "But you better hurry up and think. The line is moving fast."

There's a group of girls in front of us who are chatting excitedly and a boy ahead of them with a super-large backpack. He bounces up and down nervously until the girl from my English class gestures for him to come up to the table and he sprints over. It's endearing and makes me wonder who he's eager to send a note to. Carmen sees too but laughs.

"I have until third period to think about it, remember?" I say, distracting her. "There's a bin outside Principal Wheeler's office for dropping the hearts off."

Carmen's eyes light up. It takes me a second before I realize she's looking over my shoulder. "What about one of them?" she asks, and I turn around to see who she's looking at.

I automatically sigh. Of course it's the boys basketball team—the seniors, anyway, and a couple juniors. Pete's there too.

He always seems to have some sort of radar when I'm nearby, and now is no exception. Pete looks up from a conversation he's having with a guy from the basketball team and spots me across the gymnasium lobby. I might be embarrassed that we made awkward eye contact if it wasn't for the fact that he smiles immediately. I feel my cheeks grow warm, like they did the first time we locked eyes after a game.

After the accident Pete told me he wouldn't get back

9

together with me since I had broken up with him for a legit reason. Apparently, I had done it because my heart wasn't in it anymore. When Pete told me, he almost started crying like we were breaking up all over again. I realized then how much pain I put him through, even if I couldn't remember it. I vowed to leave him alone after that.

But breakups in high school are strange—you still run into each other and have to wave hello, even though you already said goodbye. When he waves to me now, I smile like I always do as Carmen raises her eyebrow at me.

"You know there *are* other people besides basketball players at the school," I say.

"Like who, *Turtleboy*?" she retorts, looking at the boy who just paid for his paper hearts and is now strapping his big backpack on again. He does kind of look like a turtle. Jessica and Katie laugh as I give an uneasy smile.

"Wait a second," Carmen continues. "Is Sarah Chang *flirting* with Turtleboy?"

I'm not surprised that Carmen's going to continue picking on this poor boy, but I'm surprised that she knows this girl's name. She's not the type to be on Carmen's radar. Maybe she has a class with her? The girl is handing the boy his paper heart and smiling at him—I'd hardly call that flirting. But Jess proudly shows us her phone. She took a photo of the exchange. From the angle, you can barely see the cutout. It looks like they're holding hands.

"Aw, a match made in heaven," Jess says. She even has the perfect rabbit teeth. The tortoise and the hare."

"Oooh. That's a good one." Carmen smiles smugly.

"You guys are terrible," I say, but with not enough force to actually make a difference. I see Jess typing on her phone. Before I can say anything, she looks up and gives a satisfied smile like she does when she posts something.

"So anyway, where are we getting ready for the game tonight?"

My friends start chatting excitedly again, but all I can do is stare at the one heart dangling from the ceiling. It's the same as the others but a little ripped at the bottom. I can't help but feel a little out of place, just like it looks.

Maybe hearts are like paper. Once they are torn, they can never be perfect again.

When I'm up in line, I buy paper hearts for my friends and sister, like I planned, and an extra one for Sarah Chang.

Chapter 2

A LOT OF PEOPLE HAVE ASKED ME WHAT IT'S LIKE TO HAVE amnesia.

You know when your iPhone suddenly dies and you're no-where near an outlet? Then you have to go hours feeling excommunicated from the world, wondering who's trying to talk to you, unable to look up anything.

Or even worse, when your phone breaks. Maybe it got wet somehow or it slips out of your hands and when you pick it up, the front is shattered and you pray that everything is already uploaded to the cloud. But when you go to the Apple store you learn there's no way to recover your recent photos or texts—nothing. Well, that's .01% of what it feels like to have amnesia, but that's the best comparison I have. Suddenly, there's a chunk of your world missing . . . and there's no way to get it back.

My phone analogy is ironic because after my accident,

I found out my phone was as damaged as my car. The only things that I was able to retrieve were my contacts and some photos I had already uploaded months before. I remember staring at my new, blank phone and feeling like I was starting my life over again in more ways than one.

But even that was put on hold until I could get better. Then, once I did, my priority was catching up during summer school on all the classes I'd missed.

Now it's the second semester of my senior year, and since my college acceptance emails have already come, focusing is harder than it has ever been. Today, instead of listening, I'm working on my paper hearts.

Being the perfectionist that I am, I type out everything I'm going to say on my iPad before I actually write on the paper so I don't have any mess-ups. Then I plan on writing them in a script font I've gotten really good at with my favorite pen. A lot of the paper hearts I received remind me of how yearbooks are signed at the end of the year. *Hope you have a lovely day. Have the best Valentine's Day ever! Love, X.* But I like to make mine personal. Every year I take the time to write out what I love about the people I'm sending them to.

Jessica can be super mean to other people, like Sarah Chang, but it's so ironic because she's one of the nicest people in the world if she's actually friends with you—she always has your back. Jess was the first one to come to my defense when people would ask about the accident. *Do you think she wants to talk about that?* she'd ask so aggressively it would make the other person turn red. I can't imagine her ever being disloyal.

Katie can be perceived as a pushover, but really, she just wants everyone in our friend group to be happy. She's the best person to go to for advice. When I was struggling coming to terms with my breakup with Pete, she told me if we were meant to be, we would find our way back to each other. Just hearing her say that helped me more than she knew. Everyone needs a friend like Katie.

Then there's Carmen, who gets the longest letter because we've been best friends the longest.

I start out reminding her about our best-friend bracelets from middle school. I wore mine until it was practically hanging on by a string. During those days, we were the kind of friends who were perfectly happy just the two of us. We would go to each other's houses for sleepovers, memorizing song lyrics and trying new lip gloss colors neither of us were actually allowed to wear to school yet. But when we entered eighth grade, Carmen announced that we should *branch out.* Carmen usually filters what she really wants to say, like she does photos before she posts them. In retrospect, I know that what she meant is that we needed more friends. We found Katie and Jess shortly after. But Carmen's always like that—when she wants something, she goes out and gets it.

She's really pretty, but what she doesn't get told enough is that she's also really smart. She can memorize a song after listening to it only a couple of times. She barely has to study for tests because she's so smart she doesn't need to and still gets As. I think that's why she can get away with calling other people nerds. She also gets away with a lot because she's so funny. But those are just a few things about Carmen—there's more.

Her enthusiasm is contagious and has always been what pushed me out of my comfort zone. First time sitting with seniors at lunch? It was Carmen dragging me along, insisting that nobody cared we were sophomores. My first all-nighter? Entirely Carmen's idea.

A lot of times I'm envious of how well Carmen handles the tough things in life. She's learned to be tough, just like her mom—the two of them had to be when Carmen's dad left them. When I was in the hospital, instead of crying her eyes out, she went into action and started the GoFundMe for my parents. I don't know what would've happened without her.

As I tell her this, I don't worry about being sappy. My paper hearts normally are.

I tone it down a little for my little sister, though. She probably thinks the paper hearts are stupid because I came up with them and simply because she thinks a lot of things are stupid lately. A couple of months ago she started dating this boy named Steve who is in my grade but who I'd never met. When they first started dating, I stalked his social media like a good sister would and noticed that all of his ex-girlfriends looked exactly like my sister. Thin. Straight brunette hair. The only thing that was different was that she lacked the *look*. The I'm-trying-so-hard-to-look-like-I'm-not-trying look.

Slowly but surely, she started morphing into that too. I hoped it was just because she was getting more into fashion, not because she was trying to be some girl he wanted her to be. Whenever I see my sister, it reminds me that I'm not the only one who has changed this past year. Sometimes a car crash changes you and other times a boyfriend can crash into your life too. But from what I can tell, he's a decent boyfriend. I wonder if he'll send her a paper heart. I decide to keep mine short and sweet: *I love you, little sister. Don't ever change.*

Then I get to Sarah's, which is more difficult than I expected it to be. I have to think a little harder because I don't really know her. Eventually, I decide I should just write what I love about her too.

I love the way you can pull off Warby Parker glasses, combat boots, and overalls. I love the way you answer all the questions in English class. I love reading too, but even when I think I know the answer I'm afraid of looking dumb. Sometimes you say things that I'm thinking. Other times you say things that make me want to think more, which is a special quality to have.

Instead of signing it, I draw a heart where my signature would be. I hope getting this makes her day. I feel a twinge of guilt every time I think about what happened earlier that I try to ignore. So what if Jess was mean to Sarah? Sarah can be equally condescending. I've seen her smirk when someone says something dumb in class.

But I'll always remember this one time Ashley and I were watching a Netflix film. I forget which one, but it was about high school and there was this group of mean girls, like every high school movie has. I made a comment to Ashley that I was glad our school didn't have a group of girls like that, and she stared at me for a couple of seconds before saying *if you don't know who the group of mean girls is, you're in it.* For a long time, I forgot about that, but lately I'm noticing that little things like Jess taking a stupid picture are really bothering me in a way that they never did before.

Maybe I've matured more than most people because of the accident—I know what it feels like to have everyone talking about you. It's brutal, especially when the stuff people are saying is true. I can see now that nobody deserves to be gossiped about. Life's too short for that. Part of me wishes there were paper hearts all year round that people could send to one another to say how they feel. But there aren't—I only have this one time of year, so I'm going to make it count.

I finish typing my thoughts in homeroom and then I write my letters out in second period study hall with my favorite pen. The teacher, Ms. Pearson, doesn't care what we're working on as long as we're quiet. I notice her bun moving back and forth over her desk as she grades papers before I begin writing the first paper heart.

After my accident, I spent a lot of time in my room alone. Sure, my mom would check on me once every half hour and my friends would constantly FaceTime me to say hi. But mainly it was just me.

I was supposed to do nothing other than heal—everyone kept telling me to *focus on getting better.* I heard that phrase a lot, especially when I'd try to find out what happened during those weeks I couldn't remember. But the type A in me needed to focus on something else. So I picked up something I'd always wanted to try. Calligraphy.

It seemed like the obvious thing to learn for me. I've always been a doodler. Even in kindergarten, when I was first learning to spell my name, I'd write it over and over, trying to make it perfect. Once I learned cursive, I'd sign my name everywhere like I was signing autographs. But really, I just loved writing.

But being the perfectionist I am, I always knew it could be improved. Once I settled on learning calligraphy, I ordered the supplies online and spent *hours* watching YouTube videos. Then writing. Then watching a couple more videos.

I did this on repeat for months. When I wasn't doing homework, I had my special oblique open in hand and my sketch journal opened wide. The beginning pages were just filled with the alphabet when I was still trying to figure out how to hold my pen at the right angle, but by the end you can really see how my lettering improved. I'd write anything and everything just to practice. Lists. Quotes. Random thoughts. Slowly, my hand got what my brain was trying to do, and it was okay even when it didn't, because with calligraphy, you can mess up. Even with the smallest smudge, you can start over, like it never happened. I wish life were that simple.

My favorite part about calligraphy, though, is that you get to create something beautiful with precision.

That's what I'm trying to do now with the paper hearts—make them into something beautiful that my friends and my sister will want to keep. I carefully write my messages, including little intricate flower designs for each one. They must be good, because the boy who sits in front of me never makes any noise except when he turns around to loudly crack his back in this gross twisting way on each side, and when he does that today, he pauses and tells me he's impressed. I smile until he turns to crack his back on the other side.

After study hall, I go to the bin outside Principal Wheeler's office. There's a little slot on top, and I slide my pieces of paper inside. As they fall, I smile, knowing that soon they will be folded into paper hearts. It's the only thing I've liked about today so far.

~

The student government starts passing out hearts fifth period, which is when my friends and I have lunch. Originally, Carmen and Jess had it sixth period, but they spent a day at the guidance office complaining until eventually Ms. B caved. It's very unlike her to bend school rules for anything, but Carmen and Jess used *me* as the excuse. *We want to help Ella reacclimate*, they said. It would've been nice if it were true. When they told me what they did, they were laughing like it was a big joke that I was in on. I never complained, though—having lunch with all my best friends is normally the best part of my day.

But maybe not today.

As different members of student government walk around with tote bags filled with paper hearts, my chest tightens. I love getting paper hearts, but sometimes the anticipation gets to me, wondering who decided to send me one. I spot one of my guy friends from planning committee reach into his tote bag and hand a paper heart to a girl named Jenelle. She waves it in front of her friends, who start giggling excitedly with her.

"Ella, are you even listening?" Carmen asks.

I snap my head toward her. "Er—" I start to say, but she interrupts me.

"I asked if you're going to the game tonight."

In the past this wouldn't have even been a question. I'd be the girl sitting in front with a handmade sign with perfectly drawn bubbled letters in maroon and gold Sharpie. When I was dating Pete, I always painted his number on one of my cheeks and the letter *A* for Arlington High School on the other. Games and pep rallies were a big deal to me then. I had organized a booth for student government so that before games everyone could buy flash tattoos, maroon and gold scrunchies, funny T-shirts, and beaded friendship bracelets with phrases like *Go Fight Win* or your class year.

I'd always go all-out. Freshman year I ironed different patches on my jean jacket, including my last name on the back, like a jersey. Instead of a number, I had an anchor, because that's the school logo.

This year for Spirit Week I dressed up, like everyone else, but I didn't plan my outfits weeks in advance like I used to. I just threw on the maroon and gold clothes I already had in my closet and let Carmen dust my eyes with glitter and Katie French-braid my hair with matching ribbon as Jess chastised, *I can't believe you of all people forgot about Spirit Week.*

Not to sound dramatic, but it's hard to have spirit about anything else when you've lost it in yourself.

I used to see a psychiatrist on a weekly basis, but I stopped recently. Not because of the stigma or anything—I just felt like I'd gotten everything I needed out of therapy already. Really, the only thing I had to work on was letting go of the weeks I lost. My therapist always reminded me that no matter how hard I tried, I couldn't force myself to remember what happened, and every time I got annoyed at other people for not remembering for me, I was pushing them away.

I stopped seeing her after New Year's. Holidays are often seen as a time for celebrating, but I like to think of them as a chance for a fresh start. I buy into the *new year, new me* mantra, but I think Valentine's Day could be good for fresh starts too. With everything else going on in my life, I haven't thought much about boys. When could I, when all I've been thinking about is school? Everyone around me told me to take it easy after the accident, but I wasn't about to let my grades plummet because of it.

But what if Valentine's Day is meant to be a gentle reminder that love is important too. You start seeing ads everywhere on Instagram. Valentine's Day candy starts busting out of stores. You can't *not* think about love . . . and maybe that's a good thing.

Maybe we need a reminder that it's okay to want love. If it's as great as everyone says it is, who wouldn't want it? And if I want to find it, I can't stay in my room forever.

"Yeah, I should be at the game," I finally answer.

Carmen raises her eyebrow like she doesn't know if she believes me.

"It's the *playoffs*," she says. "Everyone is going to be there."

"I said I should be there," I repeat.

Carmen nods. She's satisfied—for now. Sometimes our friendship feels like my old bracelet, hanging by a thread.

"What's taking these people so long?" Jess whines from the other side of the table. "It's like they're purposely handing out hearts to everyone but us."

"You're so impatient," Katie says. "They're making their way over here."

Surveying the cafeteria, I see that different tables have already started getting paper hearts. I spot Sarah Chang again. She digs into her tote bag and hands a boy a paper heart. He's sitting at a table with a bunch of other guys, and they all start hollering and laughing as he accepts the heart, turning red enough that I can see it from tables away. There's a bunch of oohs and aahs as he opens the letter, but Sarah has already moved on to a new table near us.

She's always been in student government but never has been part of the planning committee. I wonder what made her switch this year. She used to be the treasurer—maybe it just got boring? As she walks past our table, she looks down at her combat boots, almost like she's afraid.

"Does she not see us over here?" Jess asks, waving. The David Yurman bangles on her wrist jingle.

"I wonder if she saw what you posted," Carmen says. I turn back to the table and she's wagging her finger at Jess. "Maybe this is your fault."

Jess drops her jaw. "Don't blame this on me."

"Guys, we might not even get ours right now," I say, trying to reassure them. "They pass the hearts out for the next two weeks."

But as I say it, I feel someone come up behind me. I whip my head around. It's a boy I don't recognize—a freshman, most likely. He has small freckles that cover his nose, and he clenches the tote bag like he's nervous.

"Are you Ella Fitzpatrick?" he asks.

"Duh," Carmen says. I nod, embarrassed.

"I have a few hearts for you in this batch," he says, pulling out four paper hearts.

"Thank you," I say, taking them from his slightly shaking hand. Then he walks over to Carmen, too timid to ask her name. His tote must be filled with paper hearts for people with *F* last names. Carmen's last name is Fairchild, so whenever things are alphabetical, we get to sit by each other.

When he pulls out one heart, Carmen gives him a death stare.

"Are you forgetting any?"

His eyes widen, and he actually pokes through his bag again.

"Ugh. Just the one," he says, looking back up. He smiles, but Carmen looks away and opens her letter. She scans the page quickly.

"Just from some nerd in my AP chem class," she says, sighing like she expected there to be more. Or maybe she was hoping it was from someone else. "*That* was anticlimactic."

"At least you got one," Jess huffs.

"Oooh, look, that girl is coming over too," Katie says excitedly. She means Sarah Chang.

But once Sarah's standing next to me, Katie doesn't look as enthused. There's a red pin attached to Sarah's bag that says THERE IS NO CHARM EQUAL TO THE TENDERNESS OF THE HEART. It makes me smile since that's something I'd wear too.

But Sarah isn't smiling. Her lips are pursed in the same way they are when our English teacher sees her hand raised but looks around the room to give someone else a chance to speak.

"Here," she says, handing three paper hearts to Jess without looking at her. It makes me wonder if she knows Jess posted something. "And here are yours," she says to Katie. Carmen's still glaring, but she doesn't notice. She doesn't look at any of us. Once she hands Katie her paper hearts, she darts away to the next table as quickly as she came. As she walks away, I can't help but feel a guilty twinge again. I hope she opens her paper heart from me soon.

"That girl is so weird," Carmen declares once she's out of earshot. The other girls give each other uneasy glances, but I glare at Carmen. How does she not realize we're in the wrong here?

"You're just jealous that I have more hearts than you," Jess eventually says, elbowing her in the ribs.

"Am not!" Carmen says. "Okay, what're you guys doing? Open yours."

Just when I was thinking about calling Carmen out for being more of a jerk than usual, I open my first paper heart.

Ella,

It's normally you who is the sentimental one with these paper hearts. But now it's my turn. We've been through so much this year and I don't know what I'd

do without you by my side. I want to make this last
semester before college the most memorable one yet.
I love you more than pizza at Gino's, Bachelor
Mondays, and all the Froyo toppings. And we both know
that's A LOT.

                                    XOXO Carmen

When I look up from reading the letter, Carmen's smiling like she knows I opened hers first. I mouth *I love you too* while Jess and Katie are busy reading their own letters. Carmen reaches out to me under the table and squeezes my knee.

At the beginning of sixth grade, when my family moved to town, I dreaded being the new girl in school—but Carmen claimed me day one. She still reminds me of that from time to time. She tells me *imagine if I didn't befriend you.* I can imagine. I remember worrying the whole summer whether I'd have someone to sit with at lunch. Luckily, I totally got to avoid being the loser new girl because Carmen swooped me under her wing. Never mind the fact that she later admitted she just wanted to be my friend because I was pretty. I knew I was lucky to have her.

I'm still lucky, even though I have to remind myself of that sometimes. Because even though she can be a lot, there's a lot to love. Plus, I know deep down she's not as tough as she makes it seem and she values our friendship over anything.

Psychologists say that if you're friends with someone for over seven years, it'll last a lifetime. We're going on seven now, and that's just one of the reasons we'll be friends forever.

The other paper hearts are from guys I only sort of know. The first is from a boy named Andre Johnson who I used to do student government with. It says *Happy Valentine's Day. Planning the dance has been impossible without you. We miss your fun ideas, planning expertise, and of course, you. You're welcome back at any time.*

For a brief second, I wish I were busy calling florists to get the best deals for flowers and decorations.

The sadness must show on my face, because Carmen grabs the paper heart out of my hand and reads it.

"Who does this guy think he is?" Carmen says. "You're over student government and you can make your own decisions. Next."

I nod and read my next paper heart. It's from a boy named Greg. I only know who he is because he's on the baseball team. At least I know that much, so his paper heart makes sense.

Roses are red, violets are blue, it would be an honor to get struck out by you. —Greg

I laugh as I read it out loud. "Do you think he wrote it or one of his teammates?"

"Who cares? He's cute!" Carmen says.

Jess eyes her. "When I liked him sophomore year, you said he was too short."

"Yeah, for *you*," Carmen says. "Not for Ella. Find someone you can wear your Jimmy Choo heels with to the Valentine's Day Dance."

"Well, Miss Five Foot Two over here takes all the tall guys like Pete," Jess says. She says it staring at my last paper heart like it could be from him.

"I know what you're thinking, and no, it isn't," I say.

"How do you know? Everyone wants our high school's best couple to get back together."

My cheeks warm. That may be true, but there's no way this is from Pete. People sometimes get creative with their paper hearts, but this one is beyond. Before I can argue that it isn't Pete, Jess's long arm reaches across the table and she snatches the paper heart from me. I try to grab it back, but she's already unfolding it. When it's fully opened, she frowns.

"What?" I ask. "Who's it from?"

"It doesn't say," she says, frowning again at the letter. "It doesn't really say anything."

"What does that even mean?" Carmen asks, reaching for the paper.

"Can you guys be careful, please?" I whine. "You're going to rip it."

Carmen ignores me and grabs the letter from Jess's hands. When she's done reading it, she looks at me.

"She's right. It's from another weirdo."

"Can I be the judge of that, please?"

Carmen pushes the paper across the table to me. I read it once and then twice, like the words will magically click into some sort of meaning—but they don't. I blink at the three words that I don't understand: *Clover and Gold.*

"Oh come on. Why am I the only one who doesn't get to know?" Katie complains. I hand her the paper.

"Do you have any idea what that means?" Carmen asks.

I shake my head as Jess whips out her phone and begins to type. "Nothing comes up on Google," she says.

"Sorry, girl," Katie says, sliding the paper back to me. "I don't know what it means either."

I frown. "But, guys, what do I—"

"Just forget about it," Carmen says, then starts talking about the game tonight. But I don't care about the game, I think, staring at the watercolored piece of paper in front of me. I care about who sent me this mysterious paper heart.

~

Once the bell rings, Jess and Katie go in one direction and Carmen and I head in the other. She has study hall now, so she always comes with me to my locker because it doesn't really matter if she's late.

"So are you *actually* going to the game tonight?" Carmen asks once we get to my locker. She pulls a lip gloss out of her white leather backpack, and I get a whiff of strawberries as she puts it on in front of the mirror hanging on my locker door.

"Maybe," I answer.

She blinks at me. "Why do you always do this, Ellie? Please, for me? I've been talking to Anthony . . . and I could really use my best friend there."

"Anthony? Basketball Anthony Barbo?"

She smiles. "Yeah, I think I really like him. We've been texting a lot. I've been meaning to tell you, but I didn't want to jinx it or . . ." She trails off, looking down.

"Wow. That's great," I say, trying to sound supportive and not completely surprised since we normally tell each other everything right away. "Really. I can totally see this."

She looks back up. "So, will you come to the game?"

"I promise to think about it," I say, and I smile because I do desperately wish I could be the person she remembers. It's just not that simple. She narrows her eyes at me in a way that makes me feel like she's looking for her best friend.

I'm about to say something when the bell rings and I quickly forget what it was. I sigh.

I've been holding out hope that one day—maybe, just maybe—I'll remember why I left the Valentine's Day Dance early by myself. Why I broke up with Pete three weeks before the dance when we were Arlington High School's most perfect couple. Why I can't remember putting those three items in my secret hideaway.

But if I can forget something that I was just thinking about a second ago, how on earth am I supposed to remember all that?

"I—" I start, but she cuts me off.

"We're already late," she says. "I'll see you later."

When she leaves, I don't chase her and tell her that I've changed my mind. That of course I'll be her wing woman.

Instead, I open my backpack and look at my mysterious paper heart again before walking to class.

People like to use the phrase *on brand*, especially when they've figured theirs out. But what if you don't know what your brand is yet? What if you think your brand is one thing and it's completely different? Like when Dunkin' Donuts dropped the "Donuts" from their name but kept selling donuts? Talk about delusional.

I guess if someone were to ask me how I viewed myself before the accident, I would've said your typical high school girl who works hard but also likes to have fun with her friends. Aside from my type A tendencies, which sometimes get the best of me, I would have said my life was pretty great. On the outside, it may even have appeared picture-perfect.

It wasn't until after my accident that I realized that might not be my brand after all. Or at least, that wasn't how other people saw me.

When the news broke that I was in the hospital, more people than I ever imagined sent me flowers. When the flowers died, my mom and sister kept the cards for me in a shoe box so I could read them once I was up to it. One day while I was on bed rest, my sister came to my room to bring me water. I don't remember what prompted me to ask to see the pile she saved for me. Maybe I was in a good mood that morning—but all I remember is feeling the complete opposite later.

Ashley handed me the shoe box, and I read the cards one by one. None of them were mean, per se, but the messages behind the wording started to get to me. A girl named Sadie wrote, *I know we haven't been friends since middle school after that sleepover but I just really wanted to let you know I'm thinking about you and I hope you're okay.* I had never really thought about how we drifted apart, but she was right—we did. I'd never realized there was a real reason, though.

To be honest, I didn't even know what sleepover she meant. For the most part, my sleepovers were pretty typical. We would paint our nails with the newest Essie shades or do facial masks. We always did karaoke. Sometimes we'd play a game called Truth or Text, which is basically Truth or Dare but instead of a dare, the person next to you can send a text to anyone in your contacts. I was happy just painting nails, but my friends insisted that we play, and I, being the pushover I am at times, agreed. The game got tense, especially when embarrassing texts were sent. Carmen said that was what made it so fun. But maybe it wasn't fun for everyone?

There was another card from a girl named Alex McCormack that said *I know we've had our differences* but that she donated to GoFundMe because no one should have to go through what I did. Another from a girl who has been in my homeroom for the past three years who started off by explaining who she was because I probably didn't know. It wasn't that she intended to be hurtful—she finished the note saying that she can't wait until I'm back on my feet. But it hurt, like all these cards did. They were all heartfelt well-wishes, but to me the underlying message was that people didn't see me the way I wanted to be seen. I read between the lines—they saw me as someone who didn't care about anyone but myself.

The worst part though, was that maybe they were right.

I remember touching the bandages on my chest and wondering if I was ugly on the inside too. I quickly shoved away the thought. If my mom saw me crying one more time, she'd make me see my new psychiatrist until I was twenty. But the thing about thoughts you try to shove away is that they push back harder than most.

As I started putting the cards back in the shoe box, I vowed to be different. I still didn't know what "brand" I was, but at that moment I realized I'd rather it be anything else.

Still, rebranding yourself is easier said than done. That was months ago, and at this rate, I might as well wait until college.

I sigh before staring at my watercolored paper heart again, wondering who the sender could be. At least the message isn't like any of the get-well cards, I think, but I still have this feeling in me that I'm supposed to know what Clover and Gold means—or that I did once, anyway.

Like this mysterious paper heart shouldn't be so mysterious at all.

Chapter 3

AFTER SCHOOL I'M HELPING MY MOM MAKE DINNER WHEN Ashley comes in the kitchen to say she's going to the game with Steve and then to the Daily Planet. Normally, everybody goes to the diner after a big win, but Ashley isn't the type to go to school functions. She claims she gets claustrophobic, but that doesn't stop her from going to see weird indie bands she likes. I eye her suspiciously, wondering if she's really going to some sketch concert at the Chance she doesn't want my parents knowing about instead.

My mom looks up from the taco recipe I found on Pinterest while I slice onion for the guac. "Yes to the game, but Steve has to drive you back afterward."

Ashley's eyes blink rapidly underneath her heavy cat eyeliner and then she lets out a loud whine. "It's not fair!"

My mom puts down her knife. "How's this not fair?"

"Because you don't need to do anything. Steve is going to drive me there and back. And besides . . ." She starts looking at me now. "Wasn't Ella's curfew like eleven?"

The way she said *wasn't* in the past tense makes me frown. I'm still very much here in front of her face. But this is between her and my mom, so I'm not getting in the middle.

"Yes, but—" my mom starts.

"So mine should be eleven too," Ashely interrupts, crossing her arms for effect. Ashley has been getting into more and more confrontations with her lately, so I'm not at all surprised, but my mom's eyes widen. She opens her mouth like she's going to say something but then shuts it again, pressing her lips together. Then she pulls her scrunchie tighter. It's what she does when she's about to cave and make a last-effort Monopoly deal during family game night. I guess she's about to cave now too.

"Is anyone else going that I know?" my mom finally asks.

"*Everyone* is going," Ashley insists. "You don't need to worry at all." She uncrosses her arms. "Please? I really want to be there."

Her eyes start to glisten, like she'll cry if she has to. I know the feeling all too well. There have been so many times I pleaded with my parents because missing something felt like the end of the world. I'm ready to hear my mom ask a follow-up question, but she turns to me, putting me right in the middle, which I've been trying to avoid.

"Are you going?"

I open my mouth, but Ashley beats me to it.

"Yes," she answers for me.

I snap my head toward her, ready to argue, but when we lock eyes, hers say *please do this for me. I'm begging you.*

First Carmen and now her. They're acting like tonight is life or death. It seems ridiculous to me now, but there was a time when this game would've meant the world to me too. One of the last basketball games of senior year. Celebrating afterward with the team at the diner, where we always got free milkshakes with our meals because the waitresses would say it was another taste of victory.

"Well, if Ella goes with you, you can go. I prefer that you two stick together in case of emergency." Then she turns to me. "But only if you're feeling up to it, sweetie."

Ashley bites her tongue even though the look on her face says her thoughts are sizzling like the taco meat in the frying pan.

The thing is, you can't tell my mom she's being ridiculous or overprotective when she's gone through what she has. I can't even imagine how fast my mom's heart dropped when the doctors called to say I was in the ICU. Or how she felt waking up my dad and sister so they could all drive to the hospital together.

Ashley can imagine it, though—she lived it.

That's probably why she doesn't have a tantrum right now. I don't remember being so dramatic when I was her age, but

Ashley is the queen of using emotional outbursts to get what she wants. She nods calmly now, though, and without another word, it's settled: Ashley can go to the game and to the diner afterward . . . if I go.

~

We make it through dinner without talking about the game.

My dad is a science professor at Vassar College and my mom is a doctor with her own practice, so dinner is always full of interesting things to talk about. TV shows make it seem like family meal conversations are torturous, but ours are the complete opposite, especially after the accident. Now we make a point to come together for dinner. No phones. No distractions. Tonight, Ashley sets the table with our molcajete in the middle, filled with guacamole.

When my dad tells a funny story about one of his students, we all laugh, and my mom smiles at him, eyes glistening.

Not to be sappy, but whenever my mom looks at my dad like that, I know love is real.

They met back in college at the dining hall. My mom wrote her number on a napkin and handed it to him. He called her that same night, and they've been inseparable ever since. I know this because they love telling the story of how they first met. My mom remembers every detail, from the blue collared shirt my dad was wearing to the chocolate milkshake he was drinking with his fries. When asked the same question, my dad always says he'll never forget one thing: my mom's smile. He still has that napkin, so I guess you can say romantic hoarding runs in the family.

Chapter 4

AFTER DINNER I DASH UPSTAIRS TO MY ROOM. EVERYTHING about it looks like it came from a Pinterest board, from my bookshelf organized by color to the floating shelves on my walls decorated with plants and photos of me and my friends. It's spotless too. Every morning I make sure to line up all the pillows on the bed so they're stacked like it is a magazine shoot, which my sister loves to point out is just another type A thing about me.

But today has been a day, so as soon as I enter my room, I fling myself into my pile of pillows, scattering them every-where, and toss my phone to the side. It's been buzzing since school ended, but I've been ignoring it. I know they're texts from Carmen, Jess, and Katie. We've had a group chat called Brat Chat since the summer before high school, when we promised each other we'd be best friends forever.

But on days like this, it's hard to believe we're best friends anymore. I hate the way they were mean to Sarah Chang for no reason this morning. I hate even more that I don't know how to stand up to them.

Things between us have been different lately. I can't pinpoint why. But if I'm being honest with myself, the only thing that bonds us is this group chat that I don't even feel like responding to on most days.

The thought makes me frown. We used to do everything together. Sleepovers with Sephora face masks. Hibachi dinners where the chefs would throw food into our mouths. Tie-dye bagels on weekends after spin class. I was always the one who would rally the troops, but I haven't planned anything fun since before the accident.

That's because *before the accident* I was always trying to appeal to my friends. Organizing things that they liked to do, instead of thinking about what I found fun. And sure, I love hanging out with my friends, but sometimes I prefer to be alone.

Sometimes I make lists just so I can practice my hand lettering. Other times I underline my favorite passages in books and doodle those. My friends appreciate this hobby of mine when it benefits them—like when I make them really great signs for a big game or when I write them the best birthday cards—but most times when they catch me doodling, they say things like *are you even paying attention to me?* Or worse, *it's cute that you still do that.*

I know *cute* isn't a bad word per se, but sometimes when people use it, it comes off as patronizing. Nobody ever tells a boy he's cute for doing something he likes doing. That's why I know *that's cute* isn't a compliment.

I reach for my phone and start scrolling through all the texts I've missed. There are photos of different outfits my friends are trying on for tonight. Carmen has sent one of her in jeans and a halter top. She looks like she's going to be freezing to me, but Jess ironically typed three fire emojis underneath it. *Anthony isn't going to be able to look away*, Katie texted next.

My heart sinks. Katie already knows about Anthony? Carmen just told me about him this morning. Has this been going on with everyone else noticing but me?

I keep scrolling back through my text messages, wishing I could scroll back through time too. There are inside jokes I don't recognize.

Maybe Carmen's right. Maybe I have been missing everything.

One of the more frustrating things to find out is that I changed my password for a lot of log-ins before the accident: TikTok, Instagram, Snapchat, etc. The only things I can access are Twitter and Facebook. Apparently, before the accident, I changed my password for the apps I actually used. I always used to use Carmen's birthday, but I have no idea what I changed it to.

It doesn't really matter—it's not like I've had the urge to post anything lately anyway. I can still see photos I grammed because I'm public. There are only a few I don't remember taking, like the one where I'm at the diner with my friends sipping milkshakes, and the one of me in a hoodie with my bookshelf in the background. My last photo was just of me about to go ice-skating at one of my favorite spots, but after the accident it was flooded with get-well-soon comments and hearts.

I roll off my bed onto the floor and peel back the fuzzy rug that protects my secrets. After I lift the loose floorboard, I reach in and grab the three mysterious items—the dried rose, the Polaroid, and the key.

They're right on top because I've been staring at them a lot lately, like if I stare long enough, I'll suddenly remember my forgotten memories. But as many times as I've looked at them, I still have no recollection of receiving that rose or of someone taking my photograph. On the back of the Polaroid, it says *NYC 2/8* in my handwriting. Who on earth did I go to New York City with? It must have been an odd day weather-wise. There's snow in the background, but I'm only wearing a tie-dyed sweatshirt. Maybe I took my coat off? I reluctantly do that all the time when my friends want to pose for photos, so it's possible. But I've shown them the Polaroid and they all say they weren't with me that day.

As I stare at the photo now, the colorful sweatshirt reminds me of my watercolored paper heart. Then my fingertips run along the little brass key. The most confusing item I saved. What does it open?

When I ask my family what happened during those forgotten eleven weeks, they tell me I was busy with All Things College. Over winter break I made a pros-and-cons list for each school I was interested in, trying to narrow down where to apply. I was also buried in my intense study schedule, with cross-outs every day as proof that it actually happened. I ended up doing really well on the ACT, better than anyone I know. But it's weird to feel proud of something you don't remember doing—it's almost like it didn't really happen.

I tried to find out why I left the dance early, but nobody knew, not even Carmen. I'd know if she was lying. She does this thing where she blinks really fast. But when she says she has no idea why I left early, her eyes stay wide-open, so I believe her. I used to ask every once in a while, just to make sure, but I could sense she was getting annoyed, so I stopped.

Still, I find it hard to believe that all I did in those eleven weeks was study, even if that's what I told my parents and even if the events seem trivial to my friends. When you get to high school, people tell you these are the days you'll remember the rest of your life. That's all I want—to remember them.

I remain seated on my floor, staring at the items, trying to remember how they got there. But my head goes completely dark, like a movie theater does right before the feature, except nothing happens next for me. I hold the rose in my hand, hoping it might trigger some memory but the smell from the dried petals is so faint it's barely there at all.

I sigh. The only person who might know anything about it is Pete. He most likely gave me these things before I broke up with him. I've wanted to ask him plenty of times, but each time I'm tempted I get a heart-wrenching flashback of him coming to the hospital and holding my hand, basically pretending to be my boyfriend, because I asked for him when I woke up. He wasn't spiteful about how I had ended things with him, proving that he was the perfect boyfriend—perfect *human*—until the very end, and even after. It's why I vowed to leave him alone and never ask him about the items in my secret spot. Prying seemed so selfish—why dredge up hurt feelings?

But it's been almost a year, I think. *He's definitely over it by now.*

If I can just get him to tell me why these items were important enough for me to save, I can remember those eleven weeks. Then maybe, just maybe, I can move on once and for all. . . .

I head to my closet, selecting two outfit options—the jean jacket I made freshman year with my last name on the back and a maroon long-sleeve T-shirt that says I HAVE MORE SPIRIT THAN YOU in gold lettering. With the hangers in hand,

I head down the hall to Ashley's room, her emo music grow-ing louder and louder. When I get to her door, I knock and the music is lowered.

"One second!" she yells. Then there are shuffling sounds.

She opens the door and I enter her room, which is the polar opposite of mine. Band posters are tacked all over the walls, clothes are piled all over the floor. It looks like she just tried everything on in her closet. She's wearing a leather jacket I've never seen before and ripped jeans. She and Steve are defi-nitely going to some concert.

I shake my head. "Which shirt do you want to wear? You have to at least look like you're going to a game."

She breaks into a large smile. "Really?"

Ashley jumps off the bed and squeezes me tightly. I run down a list of the times I remember her hugging me: When I woke up in the hospital. When she graduated from middle school. When I took her and her friends to play laser tag for her fourteenth birthday. When I gave her a pair of gold hoops two years ago for Christmas. When she lost one of the ear-rings and I told her I wasn't mad, even though I was secretly annoyed.

When she releases me, she grabs the jean jacket and squeals, "I'll go tell Mom!"

Chapter 5

STEVE'S CAR IS EXACTLY LIKE I THOUGHT IT WOULD BE.
There are papers with scribbled-out song lyrics. A random
sock on the floor. His guitar sits next to me in the backseat
because his trunk is too small. It's a tight squeeze, but I try to
be grateful for the ride. I hold my purse in my lap tightly, as if
dropping it could contaminate it. I decide Steve's new nick-
name is Skeevy Stevey.

Every time a car horn blares, my heart jumps. Someone
beeps at us as Steve barrels through an intersection. "The light
was yellow," he insists.

I nod, even though I'm nervously staring at the floor of the
car near my feet instead of the road.

"Where'd you go for pizza?" I ask, spotting a pizza box
crumpled up underneath the front seat.

"I didn't have pizza," he says, turning around, but then

he spots the box too. "Ah, from last week. Forgot to chuck that."

It's official: he's even messier than my sister. How is Ashley not completely turned off by him? He may be a senior, but that doesn't excuse the rest of him.

To my surprise, Ashley doesn't even grimace. She's sitting in front of me, so I can see her reflection in the rearview mirror. When we were younger, we had unspoken assigned seats in the car—she always sat on the left side, and I took the spot on the right. We had this secret code: if she squeezed my hand three times, it meant *I love you.* Watching her now, I wish she were in the back with me, but she's up front helping Steve navigate. We're picking up one of his friends from school, but they must not be that close, because Steve doesn't know how to get to his house.

"Turn left here," Ashley says, checking the GPS on her phone.

"This is definitely not the fastest way to Jason's. It must be the long way." Steve shakes his head and lowers the music.

"This is what Google Maps is saying," she insists. "It's the left, right here."

We turn onto a road glowing with streetlights, heading downtown.

"I heard Pete's leading the team in points this year," Steve says, looking back at me in the mirror, but I don't give him a reaction.

"Cool," I say casually.

"Do you think you'll talk to him after the game?" he asks, smirking.

"Don't ask her that," Ashley says, then turns to me. "You don't need to answer him."

"What?" Steve asks, dumbfounded. "It was just a question."

"It's fine," I say, trying not to be surprised that my little sister is defending me. After all, she isn't so little anymore. But since when does she think she needs to protect me?

"Yeah, I probably will say hi," I answer, when really that's the only reason I'm going.

"What do you think of him with Molly?"

"Steve!" Ashley hisses.

"What? She doesn't know?" Steve asks as Ashley gives him a death stare.

"Know what? Who's Molly?" I ask.

"Some freshman," Ashley says. "I don't know if they're together. I just saw them together after the game last week and I didn't tell you because I don't know if it's anything."

"Oh, got it," I say. "No worries."

But my chest tightens because I *am* worried. Not because I care who Pete's maybe talking to, but because this might ruin my whole plan. Will I want to ask him about a rose he *might* have given me if he's sitting next to some new girl? I really should've thought this through.

I whip out my phone and quickly find the number I know by heart but haven't texted in a while.

Hey Pete! Heading to the game now. Don't want it to be weird but can I talk to you about something really quick after you guys win? Good luck!

As soon as I push send, I bite my lip. *Please, please say yes.*

My reaction must make Steve think I care about Molly, because he looks back at me. "You're *way* better, for the record." He cautiously looks to my sister for her approval. She looks satisfied and smiles back at me for confirmation, as if I need her to. "It's true."

"Er . . . thanks," I say.

Instinctively, I hug my ribs where stitches healed months ago and look out the window.

I watch Ashley give Steve another death stare, which says *see what you did?* I'd normally enjoy that they are fighting— maybe there's a near-future chance they break up. But I hate that they're fighting about *me.*

I'm about to tell her that I'm completely fine, when her next words stop me.

"Turn here on Clover."

Clover? Did she say Clover? *Like my paper heart?* My eyes dart to the window.

The headlights shine on two street signs. Then I see it. The words from my mysterious paper heart from earlier are now calling for me in front of my eyes. It is the corner of two narrow roads lined with stores—the corner of Clover and Gold.

"Stop!" I yell.

Steve slams on the brakes. The wheel turns and the car swerves a little before he straightens the wheel. Ashley gasps loudly. My body sways toward the window and then snaps back. For a moment, it feels like all time has stopped, until the car behind us beeps the horn loudly, making me jump.

"What was that?" Steve gasps as he starts to drive again. Ashley looks back at me.

"I—I just need to get out for a second for some fresh air. Can you pull over real quick?"

"Are you serious?" Steve asks. "I almost got rear-ended so you can get *fresh air.* You'd think you— never mind," he says, cutting himself short.

Ashley ignores him, still looking at me. I think she sees the urgency in my eyes, because she nods.

"Fresh air it is. I'll tell Jason I'm running late," Steve says, noticeably annoyed. But I don't care about his tone—all I care about is getting out of this car.

After a couple of blocks, Steve glides the car to the side of the road into an open spot. As soon as the car stops, I'm unbuckled and swinging the door open. The cold air instantly hits my face, and I feel deceived by the warm glowing streetlights around us, but that's not going to stop me. I wrap the scarf Carmen got me for Christmas tighter around my face and practically leap out of the car.

"I'm coming too," Ashley declares as she opens the door.

"No, I'm fine," I say to her. "Stay here, I'll be quick."

She frowns in a defeated way, like she used to when we were younger and I told her she couldn't hang out with me and Carmen. But she shuts the door and shrinks back in her seat.

I turn and make my way along the sidewalk to the corner. My toes are cold, but I don't even think about that, or about how I'm walking around in the dark, or how my phone just buzzed, probably from a new text in my group chat asking where I am.

There's barely anyone on the sidewalks. I spot a couple getting out of their car, but they immediately dart into a French café. I pass other little shops and a large industrial brick building with a bar normally crowded with college kids. Peeping inside, I see that the pool tables are pretty empty, like nobody dares to go outside.

When I see the sign for Gold Street, I squeeze the paper heart in my jeans pocket. I'm a block away now.

A food delivery bike reels past me, and I get a whiff of Italian food. My stomach jolts, but I know it's not from hunger. First of all, I'm full from the tacos. But second, and more importantly, I have a feeling I've never had before, like trick birthday candles are reigniting in my stomach.

When I turn the corner, I suddenly fear this is all a trick too. What did I expect to find?

As I keep walking toward the signs for Clover and Gold, the candles in my stomach snuff out for good. There's nothing there but the street signs. Besides, it's freezing. I should just retreat back to the car. Back where I know I can't be disappointed.

I'm officially about to turn around when I hear a jingle. Out pops a man on the sidewalk at the corner of Clover and Gold. He's holding a large bouquet, and the realization blooms in my mind like the roses in his hand.

It's a flower shop.

I walk toward the corner, my long legs carrying me as fast as possible toward warmth and answers. When I push open the door, a sign above it catches my eye: FRED'S FLOWERS.

This flower shop feels so random sitting here on a busy street, like a burst of life popping out in the crack of a sidewalk. I must have walked by this place at least a dozen times without noticing it.

When I walk inside, there's a man at a counter with rows of poinsettias, roses, and other flowers behind him. I don't know their names, but they look like they belong in some imaginary secret garden that I'd doodle in my notebook.

"Can I help you?" the man asks. I wonder if he's Fred, but I shake my head.

"Just looking," I say.

Maybe-Fred nods toward a row of flowers. "Orchids are two for one today. Let me know if you need help finding anything."

He sounds as bored as he looks, with his slumped shoulders and expressionless face. He opens his register like he's about to start counting money out of boredom.

"Actually . . . ," I start, reaching into my pocket and pulling out the paper heart. "I got this note—"

That's all I have to say before his eyes light up.

The man claps his hands and disappears into the back of the store. When he returns, he has a long-stemmed rose in his hand.

"For you, my dear," he says.

I know I should be grateful, but I'm so surprised that I forget to say thank you or take the flower from his outstretched hand. I stand there awkwardly until he pushes the stem closer. I reluctantly reach out and grab the rose.

"You're a lucky lady," the man says, smiling still. A stark contrast to the Fred who was bored out of his mind moments ago. It's obvious this sort of thing doesn't normally happen to him. I feel my cheeks turn redder than the flower petals in front of me.

"What is this for? Who is it from?"

He shakes his head. "Oh, I'm sorry. I'm sworn to secrecy."

"Have . . . have we met before?" I ask, suddenly remembering the dried rose in my stash. Maybe it's from this flower shop. Maybe this is not a secret haven but a spot I've been to before.

The man laughs. "I really am sworn to secrecy." Then he pretends to lock his lips and throw away the key.

I sigh. "Okay . . . well, thank you . . . have a good night," I say.

I turn to leave, and it's only when I'm halfway out the door that I realize a piece of paper is wrapped around the flower. I carefully peel it off the stem until I hold it out in my gloved hand.

It's another paper heart, with watercolor on both sides.

My hands begin to tremble as I read the message.

Dear Ella,

Call this a puzzle, a scavenger hunt, whatever you want. You'll be receiving 11 paper hearts total so you can take back the weeks you've lost. I'm going to take you to all the places you went to before Valentine's Day last year that you can't remember. All you need to do is follow these paper hearts to lead you back to your own.

Love,
Your Admirer

I stand there trying to process everything, but my body feels numb and I know it's not just from the cold. The paper heart. The rose. My apparent admirer. I feel a mixture of emotions.

I'm flattered, excited, and confused all at once. *What is happening?* my brain screams.

I flip over the paper heart and there's more writing on the back.

> *Your favorite place to get lost.*
> *F 823.7 AUS*

I blink at the piece of paper until my eyeballs feel like they're about to freeze. Where have I seen that number before? Then suddenly the second part of the letter plows into me: *F 823.7 AUS*. All the books I ever get from the library have numbers like that on their spines.

That must be where I need to go next.

Chapter 6

I DON'T TELL STEVE OR MY SISTER ABOUT THE PAPER HEART
when I get back to the car. The only thing I tell them is the new
plan: I will not be going to the game after all.

"Just take me to the library," I continue as we're driving
again. "Once you're done at the diner, or wherever you're *actually* going, come get me."

Steve smirks at the second part, so I know I must be right.

"But the library closes in like twenty minutes," Ashley argues. "And you know I can't go to the diner without you."

"I won't tell Mom I'm not going. *Only* if you take me to the
library. Once it closes, I'll go read at the café next door. They're
open late."

I feel my phone buzzing and I know it's my friends again.
I've already told Pete I was going, and he'll read my text after
the game. But I can't go—not now.

Could I be crazy? Yes. Even so, I was only going to the diner in the first place for answers. . . . Now I might actually be able to find them. I just have this feeling that the things in my room have to do with this too. I feel the paper heart tucked into my coat pocket.

Your admirer, I think over and over again, like a song on repeat.

I have no idea who it could be, but it seems like it *could* be whoever gave me the rose and Polaroid photo. Maybe they will reveal themselves in the end.

Or maybe it's Carmen. She's always the one trying to push me out of my comfort zone. Maybe she got so tired of me living like a shell of myself that she's taking matters into her own hands. But that still wouldn't explain the things in my room.

Whoever my admirer is, this urgent feeling comes back to me like it's now or never. Ashley must see it in my eyes, because she sighs. "Fine. But you have to text me if you want us to come get you earlier."

Steve shoots her a look like he hasn't agreed to that.

"I'll be fine," I say.

"I know you'll be *fine*," Ashley says. "But you're my sister. I have to look out for you."

"She's going to the *library*," Steve mutters under his breath. He opens his mouth like he's going to say something else, but he looks over at Ashley, who has her arms crossed. He catches one glimpse of her glaring at him and closes his mouth.

We sit in silence, the tension thick. I try to look at my sister in the rearview mirror. Her mouth is turned upside down. A lot of times when people frown their face looks nothing like a frowning emoji. But not my sister. Her lips form the distinct shape of a rainbow. As we pull into the parking lot, she brushes her eye, and I can't tell if she just wiped away a tear.

"Thanks for the ride," I say as Steve comes to a stop in front of the entrance.

"Don't mention it," he says. Ashley turns to me and gives me a small smile. There are no tears in her eyes. Maybe I imagined them.

I slide out of the car, ignoring the fact that my phone is still blowing up, and head straight to the library, because nothing else matters right now aside from this paper heart.

Until I see a boy through the window.

Chapter 7

CARMEN WOULD SAY HE LOOKS NERDY, BUT I THINK HE'S cute. He's tall and lean and wearing headphones, jeans, and a zip-up hoodie that I'd love to steal. His hair is in the middle of messy and neat. He's mouthing the words to a song as he scans the books on the front desk, like Rosemary normally does. She's the librarian who has been giving me book recommendations for years. Who is this Library Boy?

He looks about my age, but I don't recognize him. That doesn't mean he doesn't go to my high school, though. I didn't recognize half of the names of people who sent me flowers and letters in the hospital. That's what happens when you *think* you know everyone, but in reality you only know the people your friends want to associate with. Maybe I *should* know who this guy is. But what is he doing scanning bar codes on a Friday night? Doesn't he have something better to do?

That last thought is a little judgmental, I realize. After all, I'm at the library too.

You have a mission, though, I remind myself.

I push open the door, and he doesn't hear me walk in. He continues scanning the books and putting them into a pile on a cart in front of him, probably for reshelving before they close. I immediately see why he's listening to music: nobody is here but the two of us. Libraries are always quiet, but there's usually at least one person shuffling around or dropping something. The only sound now is the faint music coming from this boy's headphones that gets louder as I approach him.

He still doesn't realize I'm there even when I'm only a foot away from him. He's mouthing the words and moving like he's performing a live concert. I don't want to be a buzzkill, but I need his help finding this book. How do I get his attention? Do I clear my throat? Tap him on the shoulder?

I'm debating what to do when he suddenly spins around and sees me. His eyes get wide because I've sufficiently scared him, and he backs up into his cart, making the pile on top collapse, the books dropping to the floor.

"Sorry! I didn't mean to startle you!" I say as I crouch on the floor to start picking up the books that have fallen.

He pulls his headphones down to his neck and looks at me. His eyes are still wide, and now I notice how blue they are.

"What're you doing?" he asks.

"Isn't it obvious? I'm trying to help you," I say, gathering as many books as I can in my hands. "I didn't mean to scare you."

He bends down next to me and starts picking up books too as he watches me. I can feel his eyes on me.

"I wasn't *scared*," he says eventually. When he grins there's a dimple in his left cheek. I decide that we've never met— there's no way I'd forget that dimple. "I just wasn't expecting company," he adds.

"I wasn't expecting to ruin your concert," I say back.

He grins again, and the dimple reappears. I stand back up and place the books in the cart. He does the same but then eyes me like he's studying my face or something else. I look away, my face getting hot.

Then I shake my head, remembering why I'm here in the first place.

"I need help finding a book," I say, pulling out the paper heart and showing him the number. "This is for a library book, right?"

"Yeah, that's a call number. Let me look for it."

He heads into the stacks and I follow.

The library is best described as cozy. The shelves are close together, like they want to hug each other, and there are plush seats scattered around in front of them, so you can stop and read right there.

Wandering through the shelves makes me think about this article I read one time. It compared the brain to an endless library in which our lifetime's knowledge is stored. There are experiments that show that brains sometimes purposely forget things to make space for new memories to be stored. Meaning, we purposely forget things so our brain doesn't become too full. Learning that made me think that maybe time doesn't heal all wounds, like people say—we just sometimes replace memories we want to forget.

When Library Boy slows down and starts reading the numbers on the books, I know we're close. I thumb the spines with my half-painted nail that chipped when I was making breakfast this morning.

"Here we go," Library Boy says, stopping in front of a couple of books I've read before—*Emma*, *Sense and Sensibility*, and my favorite, *Pride and Prejudice*. I instantly know that's the one I want. *Your favorite place to get lost*, I remember as I grab the book off the shelf.

"Didn't peg you for a Jane Austen girl," Library Boy says.

I raise an eyebrow. "What is that supposed to mean?"

"Nothing. Just not very original. I'm surprised you aren't wearing UGG boots and yoga pants. What is the Valentine's Day version of a pumpkin spice latte these days?"

His dimple is showing, so I know he means to be funny, but I cross my arms.

"So you're saying that when something is popular it's a bad thing? If you work here, shouldn't you be telling me what people *like* to read?"

"No, I'm just saying Austen is the basic of classics. There are plenty of other options."

"Like what?"

"We're in a library. I could go on all day," he says, gesturing to the shelf in front of us. But he's not going to get off that easy.

"Start with your favorite."

"Sherlock Holmes."

I laugh. "I *have* read Sherlock Holmes before."

He raises an eyebrow, and since I don't know him, I'm not sure if it's because he's impressed or because he thinks I'm lying. "Really?"

"Really," I repeat, clutching the book. "But for the record, I do wear UGGs and yoga pants because they're comfortable. Call me basic. But since we read the same things, does that make you basic too?"

He winks at me. "Or it means we both have good taste after all."

"Okay, let's go with that," I say, stepping past him and walking swiftly down the aisle.

"You're leaving already? I was enjoying this banter we have going on. Almost like Sherlock Holmes and Watson."

"Or like Elizabeth and Mr. Darcy," I say back.

I instantly feel my cheeks flush. Did I accidentally just compare us to one of the most famous couples of all time? My embarrassment makes me walk faster toward the front, as far away from him as I can get.

It's only when I'm at the empty front desk, about to check the book out, that I realize I still need his help.

Suddenly, I hear a whoosh behind me. "Need someone to check you out? And for the record, I mean the book, not *you*, so don't get mad at me about that too."

So he's flirty *and* has bad dad jokes. For some reason, the combo makes me smile in a way I haven't in a while.

"How come I've never seen you before?" I ask. "Do you go to Arlington?"

He shakes his head. "No, I'm a senior at Lourdes," he answers.

Oh, the private school nearby.

"Where's your uniform?" I ask, eyeing his flannel shirt.

"I changed after school. Didn't want to stupefy muggles with my dashing blazer and tie."

I'm so impressed by his Harry Potter humor that I can't think of a clever response. Where's my Invisibility Cloak?

"Well, thanks for your help. I'll see you around," I say, grabbing the book off the desk.

But as I do, a paper heart drops out of the book and Library Boy grabs it before I can.

"Give me that!" I say, but he's already reading my next clue with a stupid grin on his face.

"What're these paper hearts for? The number you showed me was on one too."

"None of your business," I say firmly, grabbing the piece of paper out of his hand.

"Well, who are they from?" he asks.

I shrug. "I don't know."

"You don't know?" he exclaims. "So it's like a mystery?"

"Sure," I say, even though I'm half listening because I'm already reading the next paper heart.

Reach for the stars to bridge your mind and heart.

I frown. The other clue I solved pretty quickly from the call number. But this one is like some line you'd find on a valentine at the drugstore.

"What's wrong?" he asks.

"I don't know what this one means."

He makes a sound that sounds like a *tsk.* "You're the worst detective of all time. Your title of Watson has been revoked."

"*You* know what this means? How?"

"I told you. I like mysteries."

"In books, not in real life," I huff.

He swivels his chair away from the desk so he's fully facing me. "I'm a man of many talents. Mark Twain is a literary genius so people have forgotten that he also invented the bra strap. It's an injustice to only be able to have one thing."

"Mark Twain invented the bra strap?"

He grins. "See? I can be good at book recs and the occasional fun fact. I also solved this riddle easily and I just moved to this town." He looks at the computer screen on the desk. "And according to your library card you've lived here for years. You have no excuse for not solving this."

I wait for him to say something but he just smirks in his chair. "Are you going to make me beg?" I eventually ask.

He crosses his arms. "No, I just like the added suspense."

"I don't have time for dramatics," I say, my voice rising way past library level. It surprises us both. "I want to do this next clue before my sister picks me up, so if you know this tell me now!"

He leans back in his chair. "Oh yeah? How are you going to get all the way to the bridge from here?"

"How do you know it's the bri—" I start, but stop short. *Reach for the stars to bridge your mind and heart.* There are telescopes on the walkway bridge over the Hudson River. He's right; that has to be it.

And he's right about another thing: How on earth am I supposed to get there? Unless he can help me . . .

I normally don't ask for help from strangers, but this boy works at a library, likes fun facts, and reads Sherlock Holmes and Harry Potter. He cracks riddles in seconds. He seems harmless, in a nerdy cute way. The kind of guy Carmen would get homework from but then stop talking to after, even if I told her she was being mean.

"What're you doing after you close?"

He raises an eyebrow. "What's in it for me?" he asks.

"You said you just moved here. Now is your chance for a tour of the longest walking footbridge in America from a local."

"The longest one, you say?" He gives me a small smile like he's not convinced.

"Not to mention," I add, "hanging out with me is a lot better than doing nothing on a Friday night."

I'm playing to his weakness as the new boy in town with no friends yet. It's a low blow, but I'm desperate. He cocks his head at me like a dog trying to figure out what I'm saying before he responds.

"Well, when you put it that way, I should go just so you don't think I'm a complete loser."

I smile. "*Partial* loser it is." Then, realizing I asked this random guy to help me before I even got his name, I stick out my hand and introduce myself.

"Ella. Also a partial loser."

I'm kidding, but lately this doesn't seem untrue.

"I know, Ella *Fitzpatrick*," he says.

For a second, my heart drops. Of course he knows about me. Is there *anyone* in this town who hasn't heard about my accident?

It's only when he waves my library card at me that I realize he just read my name on it.

"My name is Andy," he tells me, shaking my hand.

But I decide I might still call him Library Boy in my head.

~

The last time I went to the bridge was in June with Ashley. My mom thought it was a good idea for me to get some fresh air and other doctors had given me the okay. It was right after I started summer school, so I thought I'd be fine going out in public. I wasn't.

The bridge was packed with everyone in town who'd had the same idea to walk along the water that day. There were families with kids and dogs. Others were on bikes and scooters, and boats zipped underneath us. I wanted to go home almost immediately, but because my mom really wanted me to start doing Normal Teenage Things again, I forced myself to stay.

I stayed in the hot sun as little beads of sweat formed on my neck. I also stayed as people I hadn't seen since the accident spotted me and ran up for a hug, pressing the sweat on my back into my T-shirt. By noon the sun was miserable—for anyone, but especially for me, since I had one of my splitting headaches. Ashley and I ended up turning around before we reached the other side of the bridge.

Tonight, I refuse to leave until we find the next paper heart.

It's a cold evening, so we're the only ones out here. There's a certain calmness to being by the water after dark.

The sky is pitch-black, but there's a glow illuminating the bridge. The horizon is just as bright from the city lights. They are tiny distractions from the real lights burning above us—the stars, which we're here to see. Telescopes are scattered across the bridge so people can look at them more closely.

If this were a date, it would be the most romantic one I've ever been on.

But it's just Andy and me bundled up in hats and gloves. When we talk, little puffs of air escape our lips, like they do now as he tells me there are over 100 billion trillion stars. It's another fun fact that I didn't know, but it makes me feel so small, walking on this bridge, just the two of us.

We stop at the first telescope and Andy peers into the lens. I move to inspect it from behind for the next paper heart. Nothing.

"I thought you've read Sherlock Holmes."

"I have. . . ."

"Then why aren't you doing what he does?"

I stare at him blankly, with no idea what he's talking about.

"You know when Sherlock Holmes enters a room, he doesn't look for clues, he just looks," Andy tells me.

I glare at him. "What is that supposed to mean?"

Andy laughs. "That you're just looking for the next clue. I think the point of this is for you to enjoy the view."

I cross my arms. "Who said I'm not? I *have* enjoyed it."

"You haven't even looked into a telescope yet. Come here," he says, grabbing my arm and moving me in front of him.

I look down into the lens pointed toward the moon.

"Wow," I say.

Through the lens, the moon isn't just this shining circle in the distance. It's close up and real. It almost looks like a ski mountain, with its craters in clear view.

"That really is incredible."

"It is."

When I pull back, I realize he's looking at me, not the moon.

"You've proved your point," I say. "Are we free to move on to the next telescope?"

He smiles. "After you."

We begin our walk to the next one, in the center of the bridge. The wind is cold against my face and reminds me why nobody else is here. I look at Andy and he doesn't seem to notice or care. He looks from me to the stars.

"Want to know another fun fact?"

I nod, noticing that he's walking even closer to me now even though we have this entire bridge to ourselves.

"Have you heard of Neil deGrasse Tyson?"

"The astrophysicist?" I ask. "My dad's a science professor. Sometimes I think he might have a man crush on him."

Andy laughs. "Yep, that's him. Hopefully your dad hasn't told you this one already . . . but Neil deGrasse Tyson says that we're made of the same particles that were forged in stars gone supernova."

"So what makes that fact *fun*?" I ask, looking up at the stars.

"Well, it means that we're made of stardust and that not only are we in this universe, but the universe is in us."

I look back at Andy. His eyes are as bright as the sky, but I don't tell him that.

"How'd you learn about this?" I ask.

He smiles. "I work in a library. I read *a lot*."

I nod. "Well, that's a fun fact. But maybe not as good as Mark Twain inventing the bra strap."

He looks down at me as we reach the next telescope. "Are you always this hard to impress?"

"Maybe," I say.

"What about now?" he says, reaching behind the telescope. I don't know what he's doing until he grabs something and hands it to me.

Another paper heart.

The next heart is at the peak of winter wonderland.

I read it once. Then twice. And then a third time. Isn't there always ice on mountains? At least around here.

Andy watches me think. "Well, what's the verdict?"

The last thing I want is to see his cocky grin when he solves another one before me. *Think, Ella.* So far, all the clues have led me to a place nearby, so that helps narrow things down.

And then it clicks—peak could refer to a *mountain peak.* What about the ice-skating rink at Mohonk Mountain House, where my last Instagram photo was taken? *That's it!* But then I frown, realizing how late it is.

"This next location isn't open until tomorrow."

"Bummer," he says, but he doesn't look too bummed. "Well, now that you're stuck with me, are you going to tell me about these paper hearts? You must have some idea who's doing this."

"I wish I did." I sigh.

He raises an eyebrow. "You're following these hearts and you have no idea where they're coming from?"

I bite my lip. "Pretty much."

"Interesting" is all he says back. I can't tell if he believes me or not, but he drops it. When he stares at me again, there's still a sparkle in his eyes brighter than the lights in the distance.

I debate telling him everything now. How I was in an accident and I feel like my secret admirer could be leading me to something important. But he looks at me in a way that's so untainted, like I'm snow at the beginning of December. There's nothing better. I decide I don't want that to change, especially since I'll never see him again after tonight.

So I don't share anything else about the paper hearts. In fact, I pretend that's not why we're here at all. We're just two strangers looking up at the stars.

"Tell me something interesting about you," I ask.

He leans on the railing, looking down at the frozen water, then at me.

"Hmm . . . you already know I love mysteries. What else can I tell you that doesn't make me seem like a complete weirdo? . . . I love going to diners. Not nice diners either. I call those *finers*—fake diners—because they're too nice. They buy a lot of old things like records to hang on the walls, but it's obvious the place is new. I like the diners that look like holes in the wall. Those always have the best fries and milkshakes."

I laugh. "So you're not a fan of finers. Not exactly what I was expecting. Anything else?"

"I've been to Disney World more than ten times."

My eyes widen. "How's that even possible?"

"I'm a DK."

I pause. "Is that another made-up word, like *finer*?"

He grins. "See? You're catching on. DK stands for Divorced Kid. One of the perks of being one is that your parents are in constant competition to be the favorite. Whenever one parent takes me to Disney World, the other one plans a trip shortly after. Originality isn't exactly their strong point."

"But more than ten times?" I ask, still in shock.

"Yep. If there's one way to put a damper on the happiest place on earth, it's letting your child be in the middle of your divorce animosity. They split up when I was six. You'd think they'd be over it by now."

"I don't know, how easy is it to get over someone you thought you'd be with forever?" I ask.

"Good point, Watson," he says with a smile, but there's a hint of sadness in his eyes.

I turn to him. "Are you over it?"

He gives me another small smile. "For a while I didn't think I'd be. I mean, if it were up to me, I'd fight tooth and nail before losing the person I love. But yeah, I think I am. In a way, it's almost easier that my parents can't stand each other now. There's no wishing they would get back together or anything."

"That's good," I say.

"But on a more positive note, I also like bad scary movies, murder podcasts, and overdone memes."

"Those things aren't really *positive*. . . ."

"True. Just seeing if you're paying attention. But they still all apply. Now, what about you? What're some things I should know about you?"

It's funny how you think you have a ton of things going for you or that you're interested in, but when you're asked to name some, all your answers feel super unoriginal. I used to be able to say I was my school's planning committee chair, but that's not true anymore so why bring that up?

"Hmm. I really like hand-lettering," I answer.

He looks at me thoughtfully. "What kind of hand-lettering?"

"Oh, nothing exciting. I mainly just do it in my notebook and I'm not very good yet. Actually, that's a lie—I'm good, but I know I can be better."

"So you're creative. I like it. What else?" he asks.

"Well, it's no Disney World, but my family likes to vacation in the Catskills," I say.

"Oh, like Rip Van Winkle? Isn't that where he falls asleep for years? There's this copy in the library that looks like it might fall apart soon it's been read so many times."

"Yes! I loved that story when I was younger, but it scared my sister. She was always afraid of going to bed in case she didn't wake up."

"How old is your sister now?"

"Sixteen. I still think of her as my little sister even though she's not so little anymore."

Andy looks at me. "Okay, what about you? What were you scared of?"

"Nothing too unusual. I was afraid of sharks after I saw *Jaws* and didn't go out too deep in the ocean for a while. But that's when I was, like, ten."

"And before the baby shark song," Andy says, smiling more. "What're you afraid of now?"

A lot of things. Never being able to get over missing those

eleven weeks. Driving in the snow. Driving, period. But what am I afraid of that I actually want to tell him?

"It's okay, Ella. I'm not a shark, but we can stick to shallow waters for now."

He then asks me easier questions. What's my favorite color? I say teal. When he asks about my favorite food, I tell him about my family's taco night. When he asks about my pet peeves, I tell him that I don't like spoilers in Goodreads reviews, when adults play teens in TV shows, or the fact that the word *pet* is in the phrase *pet peeves* in the first place, which he declares the most unusual answer he's ever heard. He then proceeds to ask me what the quirkiest thing about me is, and I say probably the fact that I make lists all the time. But he tells me that isn't that quirky, so I tell him maybe I'm not as quirky as he thinks. Andy just shakes his head like he knows I am.

Then we talk about our guilty pleasures, or kryptonite, as Andy calls it.

He tells me he has a huge sneaker collection—so many that he bets he has more shoes than me, but I'm not quite sure I buy that, between all the shoes I share with Ashley.

As we walk and talk, we take turns looking into the telescopes from different angles on the bridge until I can barely feel my face from both smiling and the cold. Eventually, we have to rush back to the car for warmth. Once we're inside,

Andy blasts the heat for us as we sit in the parking lot. It's only when our fingertips start to warm up that I finally check my phone.

There's a series of frantic texts from Carmen.

When are you leaving?

UM ETA PLEASE. I'm fashionably late and you're even later.

Get your butt over here!!!

It's the second quarter. Where are you?

This isn't funny Ella . . .

I texted Ashley. She said you're not coming?

Seriously.

Two from Pete that made me feel even guiltier.

Of course we can talk.

Did you decide not to come? I haven't seen you all night. Carmen seems pissed by the way. I just ran into her.

And one from Ashley

Let me know when you want us to come get you.

I only respond to that one for now, my fingers still needing to thaw from the cold.

Can you come in 10 minutes?

She types back immediately.

Sounds good! See you soon!

I turn to Andy. "We need to get back now."

Andy looks to me. "Even Cinderella gets to stay out until midnight. In the movie *and* the original Brothers Grimm version."

"Yeah, well, I'd never dare sneak out of the house like her, and my curfew is at eleven. Plus, my sister is picking me up soon."

"Where is she coming from?"

"I don't know, I think some concert with her boyfriend."

"Concert? Why didn't you go with them?"

I shrug. "A bunch of reasons. The main one is these paper hearts."

"You could've easily found these tomorrow."

Of course he thought I should be going to a concert over chasing paper hearts, but he doesn't know how urgent this is for me. Again I think to tell him but wind up saying something else.

"Well, I'm not exactly spontaneous like my sister."

"So you're telling me you never bend curfew? What does that mean? You're a good girl? A Goody Two-shoes? A brownnoser?"

"Coming from the boy who works at a library," I quip.

"Touché. Never judge a book by its cover. What's your reasoning then?"

"I just don't really fit into my sister's scene."

"What kind of scene is that? Have you never been to a concert before?"

"Of course I have. Just not *this* kind of concert," I say, not knowing how to explain it.

"Fair enough. Unless you were going to a T Swift concert, they would definitely kick you out with that shirt you have on."

I realize he can see my long-sleeved T-shirt thanks to my half-zipped jacket.

"What's wrong with this shirt?" I ask.

All he does is smirk. "*I Have More Spirit Than You*? You're asking to be the next viral meme."

"What happened to not judging a book by its cover? Anyway, I was supposed to be going to a basketball game. It would've been more than appropriate for that."

"So you went rogue and I'm an accomplice?"

I nod. "Pretty much."

"Well then, this sounds like a pretty spontaneous night for you after all. You're giving your sister a run for her money."

I smile. "I hadn't thought about that, but yeah, I guess so."

Andy doesn't say anything after that, but he starts the

ignition and pulls out of the parking lot. Once we are on the road, he presses his foot harder on the pedal and drives faster. I can't see the exact speed on his dashboard, but I can tell by the way the signs on the road are blurred. Suddenly, I feel my heart racing and I close my eyes.

"Are you okay?" he asks.

"Yeah," I say. "It just feels like we're going really fast."

He takes his foot off the gas. "Sorry. I thought you wanted us to beat them there."

He wasn't wrong. I did. I feel the need to explain myself, but it's nearly impossible without explaining my accident. Before I can say anything, he eases up on the pedal and looks at me. "We can go slow."

"Thanks," I say.

"So what's considered slow for a second date? Dinner?" He winks at me.

I roll my eyes, because I highly doubt I'll ever see him again. Sure, it was nice of him to drive me tonight, and a couple days ago I would have loved to meet a new boy that I haven't gone to school with since I was twelve—but now I have a scavenger hunt to follow. "This wasn't a date," I correct him.

"I know. You think I'd believe a girl like you would ever go out with a guy like me?" he says in a way that makes me unexpectedly blush.

I can't start looking for the next paper heart until tomorrow, but in that moment, I'm sad that the night is going to end.

As Steve drives me and Ashley home, I can't stop thinking about the paper hearts. I wonder who is sending them to me. Why do they want to stay anonymous, and why now? I don't know a lot of things, but the one thing I do know: I can't stop smiling the whole way home.

"Must have been a good book," my sister says, eyeing me suspiciously.

Chapter 8

BEFORE BED I SEARCH FOR A FRESH NOTEBOOK I'VE BEEN saving for Something Important. This definitely qualifies.

Once I have it, I crawl into bed and begin scribbling down the list of possibilities for my mystery admirer. It has to be someone who knows me well—or at least well enough that they knew what I did last February. Whoever it was also must be thoughtful and caring and a good planner, like me, to carry this out.

Pete—My first real boyfriend. But why would he try to help me after I broke his heart?

Adam—My first crush. I have no reason to include him other than wishful thinking.

*Carmen???—A scavenger hunt has
Carmen written all over it. But she seemed
exceptionally mad at me tonight when I
skipped the game. She didn't even send a
hundred sad faces. When I finally told her
I didn't feel like going all she responded
was K*

*Someone who really is just a secret admirer—
Welp. That could be anybody.*

I stare at my list over and over again, almost like if I do, the right answer will magically appear. Right now my heart wants the admirer to be a boy, but my gut says Carmen.

There have been other times, though, that I can't forget—like when we both got admission emails to our dream school, Columbia. I got in early decision, and when she found out she was wait-listed, I was immediately worried she was going to be devastated—but she acted like she was over it in minutes. *Whatever, I don't even care if I don't get in. I'll have way more fun at NYU,* she declared, which could be completely true.

But that night she organized a spur-of-the-moment scavenger hunt for our favorite seniors vs. juniors. I had been anxious about going because it would be a lot of girls crammed into one SUV, but I'm so glad I did because now it's one of my favorite memories. At the end of the night we were all looking at the photo evidence of who checked what off the list. *Take a picture of yourself kissing someone in the old phone booth at the Daily Planet. Take a picture of yourself getting a piggyback from a freshman. Bonus point if you get video of them carrying you across the football field.* It was a hilarious night all around, but one of the funnier parts was when our teams showed each other what we did.

I still remember being completely shocked that the juniors managed to get a photo with a teacher—one girl just happened to be neighbors with Ms. Cawfield and snapped a selfie with her in the background taking out the trash. I remember giggling with everyone until I looked over at Carmen. She was silent, her lips pressed together like she was thinking about something else entirely. When she caught my eye, she smiled like everything was fine, but in that moment, I realized what the entire night was about. Why the times she seems like she's having the most fun, she's really trying to keep it together. I grabbed her hand—the one with our friendship bracelet still dangling from her wrist—and squeezed hard, like I'd never let go.

We don't talk about it, but I know she hates that we'll all be going to different schools in the fall. Maybe she doesn't say anything because she thinks I'll follow her, like I always do. I shake that thought out of my head now as I focus on what I'm going to say.

Still, we've been distant lately so I'm not positive. I go from scanning my notebook to scrolling through social media to see if there are any boys I'm not thinking of. I'm stalking a quiet but cute guy in my physics class who liked the last photo of mine, when a new message pops up from someone named AndrewG on Facebook. I'm confused until I scroll through the feed and see pictures of Library Boy.

Wow. I didn't expect to hear from him again, especially when he didn't ask for my number.

When's your next love mystery adventure?

Maybe it's because I adore the sound of *love mystery adventure* that I type back right away.

9 o'clock tomorrow morning.

I'm planning on catching a ride with Ashley as she goes to work. I close out and continue scrolling through Physics Class Guy's page, when I see that Andy messaged me again. I don't have to open it to see the two-word response.

I'm coming.

No you aren't, I think, but don't bother responding yet. I'm too tired to come up with a witty way to say *not happening.* Tonight was fun, but I need to follow these paper hearts on my own. Isn't that the point?

As I'm scanning the list of potential admirers over again, I hear a knock on my door.

"Come in," I say, putting my notebook on the nightstand next to my phone.

The door cracks open and my dad peeks his head in. Lately, his hair has been getting grayer, but according to him that just means he's getting wiser.

"I just came in to say good night," he says. His eyes are slightly shut, like he's really tired. He must have waited to go to bed until we got home safe.

I give him a small smile. "You didn't have to stay up," I say, but he brushes his hand to the side like it's no big deal.

"Did you have fun tonight with Ashley?"

"Yeah," I say. Lying by omission was easier than this. Now I feel a twinge of guilt. Maybe Andy was right to call me a Goody Two-shoes.

"That's great, El. It makes me so happy to see the two of you doing stuff together again."

The little guilt I had before suddenly increases. "Er . . . yeah. Me too," I say. My stomach feels queasy, and I know if he keeps asking questions, I'm going to tell him the truth.

"And I'm glad you're getting yourself out there again," my dad says in a very Dad Way that makes even him smile. "But I know you don't need to hear that from me."

I nod. "No, I get it. I'm glad too."

"Can I ask another Dad Thing?" he asks.

I smile. "Sure."

"How's everything been going? Do you feel all caught up with school?"

"Yep. Nothing out of the ordinary," I say.

He nods. "Ordinary is good."

He's right. Ordinary has been welcome these days, at least until I found the paper hearts.

But I'm going to keep those a secret, like my loose floorboard.

"Good night," I say.

"Sweet dreams."

Chapter 9

THE NEXT MORNING, I TRY TO DRESS LIKE I COULD BE MEET-
ing my mystery admirer.

I have eight more paper hearts to go, so there's no chance
of that, but it's still fun to think about. Even when there are
things in your life that feel out of control, outfits are one thing
you can. Planning what you're wearing is kind of like planning
for an event. You have to think about colors that clash and
what will make the right statement.

Trying to look effortlessly pretty ironically can sometimes
take the most effort, though. Soon I've tried on practically
everything I own in front of my standing mirror before set-
tling on a sweater with black pants that are stretchy enough to
ice-skate in.

I send a picture of my outfit to Carmen with multiple SOS
emojis, but she doesn't answer. At first I see three dots like

she's going to respond, and then nothing. I hope she's not still mad at me.

I sit on my bed, waiting for a response that never comes. I tell myself to be patient. That she's just busy doing something and she'll text me any second. But I don't want Ashley to leave without me on her way to work. She started working when she wanted to be able to pay for guitar lessons. Two years later she still has the same job, and she's pretty good at the guitar too. Sometimes I think she's listening to music and it's just her practicing in her room.

When Carmen doesn't respond, I decide I'm going to have to make this outfit call on my own. *At least not yoga pants and UGGs,* I think, remembering Andy's remark before I head downstairs.

Ashley's sitting at the kitchen table, eating cereal. She nods at me when she sees me to say *good morning* as she continues crunching loudly. It would be a fine exchange if it wasn't for the fact that she's not in her usual barista outfit— all black with a hat that says COOL BEANS. Instead, she's in Under Armour, and her puff ski jacket is draped around her chair. But I guess it doesn't matter so long as she drives me first.

"I need a ride to the ice-skating rink," I say, thinking my best approach is to just ask.

She takes a sip of the milk. "Can't. Me and Steve are playing hooky and going snowboarding."

"Okay, so you're not working. Even more reason you can drive me."

I don't even bother asking her when she started snowboarding. We always ski together, but maybe this was another thing she thinks is stupid.

Ashley shakes her head. "Steve is going to be here any second," she says.

"Ashley, I need a ride! Can Steve take me?"

She shakes her head, mouth full of cereal. Her phone starts buzzing, so she shoves a last bite into her mouth before carrying it to the sink. "Not today, Ella."

I stare, dumbfounded, thinking about what to do next. Both of my parents work on Saturdays. Should I kill her with kindness? Bribe her? Now is the time I wish I had some cool piece of jewelry to offer her, but we have such different styles she wouldn't bite even if I did.

She must see how anxious I feel, because she scowls at me like it isn't her fault I'm feeling this way. "Can't you just ask Carmen?" she asks.

"She must be busy. She hasn't texted me back all morning," I say, mentally debating whether now would be a good time to start pouting. I'm not above it, especially when my plans are at stake.

"No offense," she says looking at me. "But this is an example of why you should just get over this not-driving thing."

I glare at her. "Offense taken."

"Sorry, girlie," she says, but she's not sorry. She's just making it clear she's not going to do it.

I'm about to beg. My brain starts thinking of all the ways I can say *please, please, please, please!* without sounding as desperate as I feel. I could tell her about the paper hearts, but would she even care? It doesn't seem like it.

I storm over to the key ring on the wall and take the keys to the car. They're the same ones I used to drive the car with, except Ashley has replaced my floral key chain with a retro-looking one of a mix tape. When it opens up, it fits her AirPods inside. Well, hopefully she's not trying to listen to music today, because I'm driving.

Honestly, I don't even care if she does. I can't believe her right now. Why is she being so difficult?

I make my way out to the driveway, where the car is parked, and open the driver's side. As soon as I sit, my butt is cold on the leather. I have the urge to get out of the car—and being freezing isn't the only reason.

The main one is that I haven't driven since the accident.

The car is completely stationary, just sitting here in my driveway, and my heart still starts racing a mile a minute. *You're going to be fine,* I tell myself as I'm buckling my seat belt. *It's just like riding a bike.* But I can't bring myself to lift the keys to the ignition. The ridges of the metal are now pressed into my skin from squeezing it so hard.

Once I realize this, I loosen my grip. *Get it together,* I tell myself before forcing my hands to start the car. There's a part of me that hopes the muscle memory will help me remember the accident, but it only reminds me of the last time I attempted to get behind the wheel—I couldn't leave the driveway without having a panic attack. *This time will be different,* I urge myself.

I think about turning the music on, but what if there's a song playing that makes me jumpier? Then, because I'm already panicking, I start wondering what I was listening to when I crashed. *Why are you thinking about that now?* I plead with myself.

But it's too late. I'm already thinking about that and how one wrong move in a car can send your vehicle spiraling. Horrible questions and thoughts begin to spiral in my mind. How many people crash in perfectly fine weather? How many people text and drive or goof around with their friends in the backseat? How many grandmas can hardly see but still have their licenses? The bad possibilities keep popping into my head faster than I can stop them—so quick that before I know it, my breathing is faster too. I try breathing in through my nose and out through my mouth, like you're supposed to do when trying to stay calm, except I'm anything but calm right now. As I look down at the steering wheel, I can feel my mind blacking out, like it sometimes does when I'm really nervous.

Then suddenly I go from breathing fast to feeling like I can't breathe at all. With the last amount of energy in my body, I reach for the door handle.

I'm still breathing heavily, but the second I'm outside the color returns to my eyes. I'm relieved but frustrated at the same time. Driving is my only option to get to the next paper heart unless I ride my bike all the way there. . . . Or is it?

I reach for my coat pocket and pull out my phone to message Andy my address, worried that he's going to take his time to respond since I blew him off last night, but he responds instantly.

Is this a new clue?

I reply.

No. My address.

Are you admitting I'm good at solving mysteries?

My cheeks get hot and I type back faster.

Pick me up, will you?

You don't have to be so demanding Watson. JK on my way.

I heave a sigh of relief in the driveway. Problem solved.

Not even a minute later, his Jeep Wrangler is pulling up. I reluctantly walk over to the car. When I approach the passenger seat, the window is rolled down. Andy's sitting there with a huge grin. "Hey there, neighbor."

I raise an eyebrow. "Neighbor?"

"Yeah. Me and my mom just moved down the street. The yellow house."

"What happened to the Florrises?" I ask.

"Who's that?"

"The old couple who lived there before you."

He shrugs. "No idea."

"I thought you were a detective."

"No," he laughs. "Just your driver, apparently. Get in."

~

We get to the ice-skating rink by 9:05, but those five minutes annoy me more than I'd like to admit.

I'm not irritated for long, though. I step out of the car and I'm reminded once again that this place is as close to magic as you can get. The mountain house itself is more like a Victorian fortress beside a frozen lake. Next to the mountain house is a large pavilion with an ice rink. If a winter wonderland exists, this would be it.

The morning is the best time to go. In the afternoon the ice will have zigzag marks ingrained all over it from the skaters' turns. But now the ice is crystal clear from the Zamboni.

There also isn't much of a crowd. One dad is there with his

little girl, who can't be older than three. They're standing in front of us in the rentals line. She's twirling in an adorable tutu that looks like it could be part of a *Frozen* costume. The mom is sitting off on the side, getting her professional-grade camera ready to capture this big moment.

But as excited as this little girl might be, I know there's no way her heart is racing faster than mine.

As we wait in line, I pull out the paper heart, holding it in my gloved hands.

The next heart is at the peak of winter wonderland.

"Are you going to tell me what the clue is?" Andy asks, trying to peer over my shoulder. I put the heart back in my coat pocket.

"You don't believe me that it's here?" I retort. But as confidently as I say that, I look around and start doubting myself. The far side of the rink is where my last Instagram photo was taken—the one I can't remember taking because it was during those eleven weeks. But I can tell where I was skating from the trees in the background.

"I'm not doubting you, just wondering why you're sure it's ice-skating. I did *not* sign up for cardio."

"The last time I checked, you *did* volunteer. But you don't need to do this with me—you just have to wait for me to finish so I can have a ride home."

"Oh no, I can't leave Watson hanging," he says, stepping up to the counter as the father and daughter leave.

I'm about to argue that he can drop the Sherlock Holmes act when the girl behind the counter asks for our skate sizes. I eye her suspiciously as I say six and a half. Maybe my mystery admirer told the ticket girl about the paper hearts, like they did to the man at the flower shop? But the girl hands me my skates without batting an eye. I sigh. So much for that.

We gather our skates and then find a small wooden bench so we can put them on. I string my laces together quickly, ready to hit the rink, but Andy takes his time, lacing his up like he's learning to tie his shoes. When he's finally done, he pulls the laces undone and starts over.

"Really? What's taking so long, diva?" I ask him.

"I'm not being a diva. I'm just trying to figure out if I need new skates. I think they messed up my size. These are so tight."

"They're supposed to feel tight. Have you never skated before?"

"Yeah, just not with rentals," he says with a nervousness in his voice that makes me wonder if I buy it. "What, you don't believe me?" he asks, reading my face and smirking. "I bet I can go around this rink seventeen times before you."

"You're such a *guy*," I say.

His smirk disappears. "What does *that* mean?"

I start walking toward the rink. "That you're confident for no reason."

"Oh, I have a *reason*," he says, taking a step too and notice-ably wobbling.

I stifle a laugh.

"I'll get the hang of it," he says, taking another step toward me.

"We're just walking now," I laugh. "Wait until we're on the ice."

"Don't worry about me," he says, pulling a beanie out of his jacket pocket and putting it on. If I didn't know he had never skated before, he could've fooled me. Something about him looks like a pro hockey player. Probably because of how tall he looks now. He's already over six feet, and his skates make him look even taller. But I definitely don't tell him this—his ego is big enough as it is.

"Just try to keep up. I'm on a mission here, remember?" I say.

Then I take a deep breath of the refreshingly cold air. I'm so excited I'm practically skipping on my way to the rink.

I scan the rink for any clues. The girl back at the counter didn't seem to know anything. Did anyone else? Would they recognize me? So far, I only see a custodian in the corner mop-ping up something that looks like spilled hot chocolate by the outdoor fire.

Maybe I should've paid more attention to the first girl at the entrance. She was too busy on her phone to even care that she worked at an ice-skating rink on a beautiful mountain. All

I really remember is that she had light brown hair in a long braid that rested on her shoulder and slightly covered her name badge. Only the letters *ie* were visible, which could basically mean any name: Marie, Allie, Cassie, Julie . . .

"Your brain looks like it's working a mile a minute," Andy says, making me wonder what gave me away. It makes it more annoying that he's right. "Do you have any other theories?" he asks.

"My only theory is that you're not going to be as good at ice-skating as you think you'll be." I smile, opening the latch to the rink and gliding right on.

I start going fast right away, which is ironic because I can't even drive a car by myself these days, but I just love the feeling your heart gets when it feels like it can't beat any faster—and your lungs feel fiery like your hands do by a warm winter fire. It's an adrenaline high, really, that I can't explain, and the only other thing that can probably make my skin hot like this is kissing someone. I quickly glance at Andy before I begin to skate faster.

I zip along the ice now, picking up speed on a straightaway. I love that the rink is practically empty, with only a couple of people to avoid, including the girl in her *Frozen* tutu, who has stopped twirling and is clutching her dad as if her life depended on it.

As I turn the corner, it takes everything in me to not stop skating from laughing so hard. Andy's still at the entrance, holding on to the side of the rink like the little girl who is still clutching her dad's hand. I bite my tongue so the search can begin.

I make my way to the far side of the rink, where my last Instagram picture was taken. Once I get there, I slow down, examining the edge of the rink. The outer walls are white, just like the ice below my skates, so a watercolored heart should be easy to spot, but as I move along the side, I find nothing.

Suddenly, there's a pit in my stomach. I was so sure the next heart would be here. What if my admirer expected me to get here last night and the cleaning crew already found my paper heart?

I shake my head. I have to trust whoever this mystery person is—so far, they've been leading me in the right direction. *Sherlock Holmes doesn't look for clues, he just looks.* Andy's voice echoes in my head much to my annoyance. Maybe if I stop looking hard, the paper heart will come more easily? I remember the photo from my Instagram. It looked like I was genuinely having fun from my smile. It was a candid photo, from what I could tell, where I'm gliding along with my hands raised in the air. If only I could go back to that moment, when the biggest things I had to worry about were college and planning the school's Valentine's Day Dance.

I take a deep breath and start skating again, this time faster. I glide in circles until the world dissolves. In my peripheral vision, I notice that Andy's finding his groove too.

I don't know exactly what I'm expecting to happen. Maybe for another paper heart to come flying at me like I'm an Olympic ice skater who has just performed?

Maybe for the girl from the entrance to come dashing to the rink with a box of chocolates and the next clue?

What I don't expect is absolutely nothing.

Did I read the clue wrong? *No,* I think. *This place is the epitome of winter wonderland.* I'm thinking about all the possibilities as I glide to a halt next to Andy, who I've ignored this whole time. But when he turns, my jaw drops.

His face is as red as a valentine, covered in blood.

~

After we find a mountain-size box of tissues, Andy tells me his sob story over hot chocolate by the outdoor fire. Thank goodness it was just a bloody nose, which often looks way worse than it actually is. Normally, I would have more sympathy, but I'm here to find my next paper heart and this is slowing me down. I want to chug the hot chocolate in front of me to move things along, but I can only take little baby sips without burning my tongue.

"It was the little *Frozen* girl's fault," Andy explains across the table. "She skated right in front of me and I tried to get out of the way so I didn't pummel her and then I ran straight into her dad, who was trying to rescue her. But then once I was bleeding, she started laughing at me like she knew what she was doing. That girl is an Elsa, *not* an Ana."

I just shake my head. I'm half listening, thinking about where to check next at the same time. Maybe I should search the cubbies in the corner.

"What?" he asks defensively.

"Nothing," I say, turning my attention back to him. "It's hard to take anything you say seriously with tissues coming out of your nose."

"I'm a *hero*," he says. "This is a *battle wound*. Harry Potter. All the Marvel superheroes have had them. It's too bad I won't get a scar. Chicks dig scars."

Not on myself, I think.

"A bloody nose is hardly a battle wound," I say instead. "And are you done bleeding yet? I'm trying to be nice here, but I still have a paper heart to find."

"Thanks for your concern, Ella, but I'm not the only one holding us up here. *You're* not even close to finishing your hot chocolate."

I look down at the large mug in front of me. It's still hot, but I pick it up and take another sip of the foamy top layer just to speed things up.

"My conversation is that bad, huh?" Andy asks flatly, but his eyes say he's joking. "Or is it the blood?"

"Both," I deadpan. Some people might find my sarcasm mean, but Andy grins in a way that makes me forget what I'm doing for a second. I take another sip of the hot chocolate and burn my tongue again.

As if he's trying to redeem himself from his poor ice-skating performance, Andy blows on his chocolate and takes a sip while pinching his nose with his other hand.

"Pretty impressive," I say.

"Is that a semi-compliment from you? I'll take it."

I laugh, and for a second it makes me forget all about the paper heart. Okay, not quite—the thought is still nagging me.

"Let's play a game to distract you," Andy says, like he can read my mind.

"What kind of game?"

"A people-watching game," he says, smiling.

"Sounds creepy," I reply, in part because it *does* sound creepy but mostly because I want to get this show on the road. The point of him coming was *not* to hold me back.

"First of all, it isn't nearly as creepy as these paper hearts," he says. "Ever wonder if you have a serial killer on your hands leading you to your death?"

I roll my eyes. "Yes, someone like that would really want to break into Arlington High School to deliver a paper heart."

"Wait a second. I thought you said you didn't know who was sending these?"

"I don't, only that I got the first one in school."

Andy's eyes widen. "How can I be your detective if you don't give me all the clues, Ella?"

I put down my hot chocolate. It clinks on the table. "Can you just tell me this theory already?"

"I thought you'd never ask," he says sarcastically. "Okay, so the theory is you can tell how much someone loves somebody by the Hot Chocolate Test."

I squint my eyes. "Go on."

He drops his tissues and smiles widely like he's fully excited about what he's about to disclose. "It's all about how they drink their hot chocolate. Take that couple, for example," he says, pointing his finger on the table diagonally to the two people sitting on a stone bench by the fireplace. To me, they look like your average couple. The girl looks effortlessly cool in patterned leggings and a puffer vest, only I'd give her the benefit of the doubt and bet that she didn't try on everything in her closet this morning like I did. She's sitting next to the guy and talking.

"I don't get it," I admit, wondering where on earth this is going. "What am I looking for?"

"You don't see it? She's paying more attention to her marshmallow than her fellow."

I glance back at the couple. It's a stretch—she looks like she's just drinking her hot chocolate to me.

"Now look at him," Andy says, watching my eyes. "See how when he takes a sip, he doesn't take his eyes off her?"

Even though I think this is ridiculous, I want this game to be over, so I do as Andy tells me to. Only when I do, I realize he *doesn't* take his eyes off her and Andy's observation is right. Still, the Hot Chocolate Test sounds like a stretch.

"So what does that tell you about their relationship?"

He eyes me intently. "You really want to know?"

"Isn't that the point of the game?" I ask, confused—why is anything with the words *hot chocolate* getting taken this seriously?

"I'm not sure your romantic heart can handle the truth."

I groan. "Please just mansplain your theory to me so we can get this over with."

There's a long pause, and I'm not sure if it's because he's debating whether or not to tell me or because he really doesn't have a theory and he's just thinking about what to say now. That's the vibe I've been getting from him lately—that he's making everything up as he goes along. The guy who will just chase paper hearts with some girl he barely knows for the entertainment of it. He's the complete opposite of me, who overthinks everything, including why this long pause is taking so long. I'm about to open my mouth when he finally does.

"The way they're drinking their hot chocolate tells me a lot of things, as does their body language. Right now, he's the nice guy who dotes on her every word, but eventually he'll grow tired of being taken for granted and break up with her. She'll be heartbroken and beg for him back. Maybe he'll take her back or maybe he'll realize there are more important things than a pretty face and find someone that wants to look at him while she drinks hot chocolate too. There are just some people who love the idea of love but not love itself."

I blink at him uncontrollably. "Geez. All that because she was trying to get a marshmallow?"

"Yeah, when there's a guy that's sweeter right in front of you."

I roll my eyes. "What has made you so incredibly jaded? Did some girl break up with you or something?"

His eyes blaze like I hit a nerve, and I have the instinct to apologize immediately until he shakes his head at me. "No, but I'm just not the type of person who follows some paper hearts aimlessly over town."

He grins, but I don't grin back. It's a low blow and he knows it.

"Oh come on," he starts, but I'm already getting up. I don't care about what he has to say to me next or that I haven't finished my hot chocolate or that he got a bloody nose, because suddenly it feels like he deserved it. I stomp toward the exit.

"Wait, Ella," Andy says, following me. "I didn't mean it like that. I like that you have hope someone is really out there doing a romantic scavenger hunt for you. It's endearing. You really are a glass-half-full kind of girl."

I shoot my head around. "You don't know anything about me."

My words are harsher than I mean them to be. His grin

fades fast, and I think about apologizing. After all, he doesn't know about my accident or why this is so important to me.

I have the thought now to tell Andy about everything. If I don't, I'm lying by omission, right?

But as I open my mouth, I can't bring myself to say anything. Maybe it's because I'm secretly enjoying this banter we have going on. It's silly. It's fun. Opening up about something serious would be a buzzkill—or at least, it feels like it could be.

Besides, everyone I know tells me it's so great that I'm moving on. Isn't talking about it taking a step back?

Something tells me these are just excuses. But if I tell him I was in an accident, he'll ask about the accident itself. It's only natural. But then I can't even answer the question—because I don't remember what happened. I don't remember this huge thing that feels like the catalyst for my life. I get this feeling in my stomach—maybe it's anger.

Or maybe it's the same stupid feeling I have when I don't know the answer to a question in class. Either way, every time someone tries to talk about it, I feel like I'm in class and don't want to be called on. So I shrink down and avoid eye contact at all costs.

I look away now, and as I realize what I'm doing, the answer slides into my brain like it's on ice skates.

The next heart is at the peak of winter wonderland.

I was right about Mohonk Mountain being a winter

wonderland, but I've been so focused on going back to the location of my Instagram photo that I completely misinterpreted the other part. Peak isn't just referring to the mountain—it's literally saying the highest part of the mountain.

I yank my skates off before grabbing my boots from the cubby. "Where are you going now?" Andy asks.

"I was totally wrong before. We need to go to the highest peak. I need a map."

"There was one at the entrance," Andy says, taking his skates off now too.

After I put my boots back on, I rush over to the front desk with Andy trailing behind me. Then I grab a map and begin scanning the different trails.

"There," I say with my pointer finger on a black dot with a tower off the high ledge. "That's where we need to go."

~

"So, are you going to tell me why you blew up back there?" Andy asks.

We've been walking in silence up the mountain. My boots aren't made for hiking, especially since these trails still have snow on them. I slip a little when Andy calls me out—I forgot that I overreacted. But of course Andy wants to remind me.

"It was nothing," I say. "I was just irritated you were type-casting me again."

"Typecasting you?" he spits out, a little breathless from the steep incline.

"Yeah," I say.

"Well, what did you mean by *I don't know anything about you*? I'm trying to get to know you here."

I know my cheeks turn super red in the cold, but they must be even redder now. My eyes shift from him to the view. You can see everything from up here—the mountain house where travelers stay, the ice rink. When I look back at Andy, I still don't know what to say.

But then, behind him—I see something up ahead. A wooden tower that you can only reach by crossing a short footbridge. From this angle, it appears as if it's floating in the sky. I forget all about my poor choice of footwear and sprint toward it.

"Be careful," Andy yells from behind me.

"What are you, my mother?" I retort back as I keep running toward the bridge. But when I reach it, I slow to a walk and feel Andy catch up behind me.

As soon as I enter the wooden tower, I cover my open mouth with my hand. There, dangling from the pointed top of the ceiling, is a long ribbon. At the end is my next paper heart.

I turn around to Andy. "I guess it's not a bad thing being a glass-half-full kind of girl," I say smugly.

But when I pull the heart off the ribbon and read the message, my smile disappears.

Chapter 10

PEOPLE ALWAYS ASK WHAT IT'S LIKE WAKING UP IN A HOSPI-tal when you don't remember what happened. Nosy people, that is—that's why I don't feel bad giving a generic answer. Something simple, like *it was scary.* Or *it was like an out-of-body experience.*

But the truth is, when I woke up, I didn't really believe what was happening to me.

The first thing I remember is the pain, but I'll skip the gruesome details. Second is my parents at the side of my bed telling me I was in an accident after the Valentine's Day Dance. They didn't know I couldn't remember the dance yet—not until later, when I was asking for Pete. The third thing is my hands.

When I first woke up, I couldn't move my body much, so I spent the first couple days in the hospital bed looking at my hands. A nurse saw me staring one day and told me that the little piece of plastic attached to my finger was called the pulse oximeter. It was used to measure oxygen in my blood. I thanked her, although it sounded more like a moan. But she had been mistaken—I wasn't looking at that piece of plastic or the machine I was hooked up to.

I was examining my bare fingernails. It didn't add up. There was no way I went to a dance with unpainted nails—Carmen wouldn't have let me. I remember feeling like I was in some bad sci-fi movie. These people by the side of my bed were pretending to be my parents.

This of course was paranoia, most likely caused by the painkillers. I later found out that doctors take nail polish off patients before surgery, which explained why I wasn't wearing any. But when I was first staring at my hands, they were like proof to me that I couldn't possibly have been in an accident after the dance. Except as I told my parents I didn't believe them, they looked at me with the same concerned expression that Andy has now while driving to the next paper heart.

You paint the gown red
(Ask for Sydney)

I pull the paper heart out in the car and read it again, even though I instantly knew where I needed to go—"paint the gown red" is one of my favorite Essie shades, and Carmen and I always go get our nails done at the same spa before big events. This includes our first day of high school, before her sweet sixteen, and before any kind of dance. In Carmen's eyes if you forget to do your nails, you might as well be wearing sweatpants. That's a little extreme if you ask me, but as judgmental as that is, I always do enjoy getting ready with Carmen—sometimes it's the small things that make a big event fun. We used to *beg* our moms to take us, and then by the time we could drive, it was a full-fledged tradition.

When Andy pulls up to the entrance of the inn where the spa is, he's facing me with a furrowed brow. "Thanks for the ride . . . really," I add, because even though he thinks I'm ridiculous for chasing these hearts, he has helped me so far. Now it's time to do this on my own.

I've been to this spa hundreds of times before the accident but never once afterward. I considered coming back to see if it would help reignite my memories, but I chickened out. The doctors said the chances are slim to none anyway, and the thought of returning felt eerie, like it is now.

"I should go before I lose the nerve," I say, unbuckling my seat belt.

"Lose your nerve? Why're you nervous? You look kind of freaked out."

I don't respond because I don't even know why I'm nervous. Maybe it's just because the thought of being back where

I was the day of the accident is a little unnerving. The girl I was then must have been excited to go to a dance with her best friend. She had no idea what was about to happen to her that night.

"Do you want me to wait for you?" he asks. "Really, it's no problem, I'm not working today. I took the day off."

Suddenly, I feel a twinge of guilt. Did he take the day off to be with me?

"Don't worry," he says like he can read my mind. "Someone covered for me. Sarah Chang, do you know her? She goes to your school."

I wince at Sarah's name but then nod, feeling guiltier than ever. Sarah's working an extra shift because I needed a ride.

"Well, thanks for the offer," I start to say. "But my sister is coming to get me."

This is true. I texted her on the way and she's getting me with Steve on their way back from snowboarding. Maybe she agreed because I sent her a bunch of SOS emojis in a row. Or maybe she did feel guilty about not taking me this morning.

"Oh, okay," Andy says softly, like he's disappointed. He grips the steering wheel tighter, like he doesn't want to let go.

"For the record, I'm sorry about what I said back there. I can tell whatever you're looking for must be important," he says, gently touching my elbow.

His eyes are sincere and it makes me want to explain *why* it's so important. But how do I even begin? I'm about to try

113

when he removes his hand to press a button by his window. There's a loud click from the door unlocking.

"Was almost going to trap you in here with me." He winks.

I laugh. "Almost worked. But yeah, I should actually go now. Thanks for not holding me hostage, and for everything."

"Don't mention it. I hope everything goes well."

"Me too," I admit.

He smiles as I slide out the door, heading to the entrance of the building without looking back. The inn is in the middle of nowhere, which is why people from NYC like to stay here for quaint weekend getaways. But the spa is open to everyone, not just guests, and I'm glad for that. It's one of those places that doesn't look like much from the outside. But when you enter, it transforms into a hidden oasis. I swear they do that on purpose to trick people so it's never crowded and always a soothing experience. As soon as I open the door, I'm hit with the calming scent of lavender.

See? This is supposed to be relaxing, I tell myself. *This is going to be fine.*

I wipe my snowy shoes on the doormat before heading to the front desk off to the right. When I do, I'm greeted by a woman with rosy cheeks and long shiny jet-black hair. "How can I help you?" she asks when I'm standing in front of her. The desk is covered with pamphlets of all the spa services—massages, facials, you name it. But I'm not here to browse.

"I'm . . . I'm looking for Sydney," I say, repeating what

the paper heart said. Once the words escape my mouth, I realize how ridiculous they sound. I don't actually have an appointment—there might not even be a Sydney that works here.

But the woman looks at the computer on her desk like she knows who I'm talking about. For a moment my heart speeds up, until she frowns. "Name, please," she says.

"Ella," I reply softly, realizing that I could be completely wrong after all. "Ella Fitzpatrick."

The second I say my full name, her head snaps from the computer to me. Her rosy cheeks instantly pale. "Just one moment," she says. There's a phone on the desk that she lifts now as she presses a long fingernail to the screen.

"Ella Fitzpatrick is here to see you," she says after a couple of seconds. It must be Sydney. I can't hear what she says back on the other end, but the woman with the jet-black hair nods. "Yes, absolutely," she says before she hangs up. Then she turns back to me, her expression now warm. "Sydney will be with you in just a moment. Please take a seat."

I raise my eyebrow. How did I go from almost being turned away for having no appointment to this?

As I head over to the velvet couch, I can't help but think about who my admirer is again. It seems like Carmen's still my best bet. She can be a force when she wants something. The GoFundMe account is a good example of that. Besides, if not her, who could it be?

I try to remember all the possible admirers I wrote down in my notebook aside from Carmen, but for some reason I'm drawing a blank, like I do sometimes when I'm anxious. I suddenly feel light-headed and am relieved to sit down. Across from the couch there are magazines to peruse while I wait, but I don't currently care what hairstyle is trendy right now or what celebrity is dating who.

I'm sitting here for what feels like forever, which is probably more like ten minutes, when a woman with short red hair pops out of the glass door. She rushes over and hugs me like she knows me. As she lets go and sees my face, her eyes are all wide, as if she's messed up already.

"You must be Sydney," I say with a smile.

"Yes, dear," she says. "I'm sorry for coming on so strong. I've just been waiting for you to come back for a while now. . . . When I heard you might finally be ready . . ." She trails off in almost a wistful way.

"You've been waiting for me?" I ask. "Who told you I'd be coming?"

"Oh, come on now. You know I can't tell you that. I'm sworn to secrecy."

Fred from the flower shop said the same thing. *I'm sworn to secrecy.*

Who are they protecting?

I nod so she knows I understand, but really I don't.

She gives me a small smile. "Let's get started with your mani-pedi."

~

I skim the nail polish rack, paying as much attention to the names on the bottles as the actual color. Adore-a-Ball, Diamond in the Cuff, Sole Mate. Eventually, I settle on Paint the Town Red for my hands and Scavenger Hunt for my toes, which seems extremely fitting.

As I hold the bottles in my hand, I realize one thing. Sydney may be sworn to secrecy about my admirer, but she may still be able to tell me about the last time I was here before the accident.

I sit in silence as Sydney fills the tub. Normally, the sound soothes me, but now the rushing of the water makes my questions rush to the brim of my mind too. Once she turns the knob off, I can't hold them in any longer.

"Do you remember anything about that day?" I ask. I don't have to specify what day I'm talking about. The way she bites her lip now tells me she knows what I'm asking.

Sydney grabs one of my feet out of the tub and begins to file my toenails before looking up at me from her stool.

"I had a feeling you were going to be curious." She eventually sighs. "And I really wish I could remember more."

You and me both, I think. There has to be *something* she remembers.

"Well, was there anything Carmen and I were talking about?" I ask.

"Carmen?"

"Sorry, the friend I was with," I answer.

She shakes her head. "I've seen you here with another girl before, but that day you came alone."

Alone? Why wouldn't Carmen have come with me? That doesn't even make any sense.

She must see the confusion on my face, because she offers a small smile.

"I do remember one thing," she says, dipping my foot back in the water and grabbing the other to file. "You were texting some boy even while I was trying to give you a manicure— that's why I remember it."

A boy? But I broke up with Pete three weeks before the dance.

"Was his name Pete?" I ask.

She shakes her head. "I wish I knew, darling, but we didn't talk about it. I was just worried about you not messing up your nails with all the texting."

I nod. "Sorry for being a brat on my phone while you were trying to work. You must have thought I was really rude."

"Oh, I didn't think that. No," she says, looking at me with a glimmer in her eyes. "Actually, I thought you were just in love."

"That can't be right," I say, mainly because I know I've never been in love—not really. But also because Pete and I had been broken up by then.

She shrugs. "You asked me what I remembered, darling. I wouldn't lie to you about that."

With that, I'm left speechless. I sit through the rest of my pedicure in pure shock. As she paints my nails with Scavenger Hunt, all I can do is wonder why my admirer wanted me to come here. Was it so I could hear that?

After my manicure, I'm so dazed, I don't even realize that I'm leaving the spa without a new paper heart.

Chapter 11

CARMEN DOESN'T TEXT ME BACK THE WHOLE WEEKEND. AT first I try to pretend that she just didn't see my message . . . but I know she's glued to her phone if she's talking to Anthony, so it's official: Carmen's ignoring me.

I can't remember the last time she was this mad at me. She's been annoyed at me before plenty of times—whenever I can't have a sleepover because my parents want to have a family game night, or that time I refused to coordinate our outfits for Spirit Week because I already had put together one for myself. Even when I accidentally revealed her crush to another friend in the eighth grade, she got over it.

But she has never gone on a full-on texting strike . . . especially not when I need her the most.

I have so many things I want to say to her. *I've asked you about the night of the dance before and all you said was you didn't know why I left early. Why did you conveniently leave out the fact that we didn't even get ready together? Were we fighting? Did I leave early because of you? Is that why you won't tell me . . . do you feel guilty?* Whenever I begin to text these questions, I can't bring myself to push send.

My biggest question for her, though, is about what Sydney said at the spa about being *in love.* Was it with Pete? Was that possible, when we had broken up three weeks before?

If I was being honest with myself, while Pete makes the most sense, he also doesn't.

When Pete first told me after the accident that I'd broken up with him, he'd said the reason I gave him was simple—my heart wasn't in it anymore. But coming to that realization wasn't so simple. In fact, as he said it, I was proud of my past self for finally putting to words the feelings I'd been having for a while . . . the ones I tried to push away.

People at school always call Pete by his full name because Pete Yearling rolls off the tongue. To me, though, he was just Pete. Everyone would say we were the *it couple,* or *goals.* But to me we were just us.

The first time I officially talked to Pete was after a basketball game at the diner. I didn't even think he knew who I was at the time. *Did you have fun?* he asked me. It was such a striking question to me. He was the one who'd played his heart out, and he was checking to see if *I* had enjoyed myself. It was the first of many moments that proved he was different.

Pete is kind and selfless, unexpectedly so for being Pete Yearling—people would still like him if he wasn't. He has this happy glow to him all the time, but I guess I'd be happy too if I was as good at everything as he is and everyone liked me. But why did they like him in the first place? There's just something about him that you can't dislike. Maybe it's because he's the opposite of egotistical and can make people feel special, like he did with me that day after the game, when he's the real star.

But as much as everyone likes Pete, could I honestly say I loved him? When I was with him I felt really comfortable . . . like a caterpillar wrapped up in a cocoon, but I was constantly waiting for butterflies.

Maybe our breakup was some sort of catalyst, though. Maybe it took setting Pete free to realize I really did love him. People say that can happen sometimes. The classic *you don't know what you have until it's gone.*

I also knew a couple of things about Sydney. One, she could be exaggerating. And two, she could be flat-out wrong—maybe I wasn't in love with anyone. Maybe I was just excited to go to the dance and I was texting someone in the nervous, giddy way you get when you're first talking to someone new, like Carmen is with Anthony. Or maybe the person I was texting *was* Carmen, and she had some logical reason why she couldn't get her nails done with me that day—a dentist appointment or something. I bet it's that simple, and the only reason my mind keeps racing all over the place is because she's giving me the silent treatment.

The worst part is that I can't exactly tell her I need her right now. I can see her just rolling her eyes at me and saying *isn't that ironic?* in the sassy voice she has perfected. She'd be right—the whole reason Carmen's mad at me is because *she* needed *me* at the game. She had asked me to go with her, and I completely bailed.

I know I screwed up, which is why I'm surprised Monday morning when a one-word text appears under my rows of apologies.

Outside

I open it while I'm sitting at the breakfast table with my mom, eating cereal, and I crunch hard in shock. Then I sigh in relief. Carmen has driven me every single day since the accident, but I was worried since she was ignoring me. I was just about to ask my mom.

"Is everything okay?" she asks me now as I get up quickly to clear my cereal away.

"Yeah," I say, rushing over to dump my leftover milk in the sink. "Carmen's here. Don't want to keep her waiting."

She eyes me. "Okay, just checking. You seemed a little *distracted* this weekend."

I smile. "I was just trying to finish *Pride and Prejudice.*"

After the last paper heart, I locked myself in my room the

rest of the weekend. As I reread my favorite book, I was reminded why I love it so much. The characters. The sarcasm. The will they/won't they love. I even enjoy how the chapters are broken up with letters—it makes me wish people still wrote them today. How great would it be to get one in your mailbox? I guess it's not so different from receiving these paper hearts.

But as I started flipping through the pages, I realized something else I absolutely adore: someone had underlined their favorite passages and doodled on the pages, just like I do. My favorite is a pair of heart eyes when the reader meets Mr. Darcy. In other places, there are reactions and questions. At first, I examined the handwriting, hoping I'd recognize it, but it's inconsistent. Sometimes it looks like the person was reading the story in a hurry; other times there's a thoughtful note. In a couple of places, when they liked a quote, they would write it out in the margins. When I got to one, it felt like it was directed to me.

Think only of the past as its remembrance gives you pleasure.

I read it over and over again. It was almost like they were telling me to stop beating myself up for not remembering—it's not going to improve my future.

I wish life was more like books and someone could write margin notes for you along the way.

But I don't tell my mom this, like I don't tell her a lot lately. She smiles at me now, gently. "Just wanted to check and make sure nothing happened at that game. I know people can some-times be insensitive about the accident."

I cringe at the word *check*. My mom is what I call a checker. She's never worried per se, but she likes to check up on peo-ple. It's probably what makes her a good doctor. If I'm look-ing flushed, she'll check my temperature. If I'm just hangry or in a weird mood, she'll ask me if there's something more going on and examine my face to see if I'm telling the truth. If she's squinting, it means she doesn't believe me. When I drive places I've never gone before, I'm supposed to tell her when I've arrived. All pretty standard Mom Behavior.

But after the accident, her checking turned a full 180. It was way too much. I couldn't leave the room without her smothering me. Eventually, my psychiatrist thought it would be a good idea for me to bring her to a session to tell her how I was feeling. She made more of an effort after that. But every so often, she does her routine checkup with me. *How are you doing? Any headaches recently?* At least it's feeling like things are going back to how they used to be.

Sometimes I wonder what's going to happen when I go off to college. Will she expect to "check up" on me every day? But I guess we'll cross that bridge when we get to it.

It's weird. College is something I used to obsess about all the time. But now that I'm in, I wish I could hold on to high school just a little longer. Maybe that's why when my psychia-trist suggested a gap year to take care of myself before being thrust into a stressful environment, I seriously considered it. Or at least on some days. The others, I think my mom put him up to it.

I shake my head. "I promise nothing happened at the game."

Because I didn't go, I think. But lying by omission is best. She'd be way more worried if I told her I was chasing paper hearts. I could see her mind jumping to worst-case scenarios like a stalker or serial killer because of all the criminal podcasts she listens to. It reminds me of what Andy said. I still can't believe how jaded he is, even if some girl did break up with him. Maybe it has more to do with his parents' divorce. But as frustrating as he is, I can't think about that right now. I have bigger things to worry about.

Carmen barely looks away from the steering wheel when I say hi to her.

After Ashley and I buckle our seat belts, Carmen peels out of our neighborhood without talking, so we sit there quiet too. Carmen's fingernails are short, which means she has been biting them. That's how I know she's really anxious. She only messes up her nails if something is chipping away at her too.

Say something to make this better, I think.

My eyes find Ashley's in the rearview mirror. She shrugs at

me as if to say *what's going on with you two?* I haven't told her Carmen's mad at me, but it's blatantly obvious now. Her lips are pressed together in a straight line. The music is off. The only sound comes from her jagged fingernails tapping on the steering wheel.

"Carmen—" I start, but she cuts me short.

"You know, the last time you started acting like this was right before the accident."

I stare at her in disbelief. "What . . . what do you mean?"

"You know exactly what I mean. Saying you'll do something and then completely bailing last second without a good reason. Wanting to do things without me and acting all innocent about it after. Were you even thinking about me at all when you decided not to come to the game?"

I open my mouth, but suddenly it feels dry, like cereal without milk, and instead of words coming out, my lips just form an O like a Cheerio.

"Exactly," Carmen says, shaking her head. "Did you think about Pete either? He told me you texted him too. He was worried that you stopped responding and never showed up. We *both* were worried," she says, gripping the steering wheel tight. When we come to a red light, she turns to me. There's a glimmer in her eye.

"Sometimes it's like you don't even think about what we went through after the accident."

That's not fair! my brain screams. I think about the accident all the time. But do I think about what other people went through? Maybe not enough.

Carmen's words are laced with pain, and after she says them it feels like the little string in me that was tying everything together is suddenly undone. I sit in the passenger seat silent, in shame. I can't even bring myself to look in the rearview mirror at Ashley, who probably feels the same exact way as Carmen.

The light turns green and Carmen starts to drive again, but I still feel like my body is in slow motion.

"You can't go radio silent like that, El," Carmen says, more gently now. "Especially not to me and Pete. We were by your side during the absolute worst. . . . We can't bear to do that again."

My cheeks flame. They were worried I'd been in another accident—no wonder Carmen is upset with me. I didn't even think about that when I decided not to go to the game.

"I'm sorry for bailing," I say. "I wasn't feeling up to it, but I should've let you know that. I'll apologize to Pete today too."

"Good" is all Carmen says back, but I let out a sigh of relief. This is a million times worse than the time I revealed her crush in eighth grade, but we're still best friends and she'll get over this.

One thing is for sure, though: I can cross Carmen off my list of suspects.

Now I really need to talk to Pete.

As soon as we all walk inside, I head toward Pete's locker instead of my own. Carmen and Ashley nod at me like they know what I'm doing, but that isn't possible, because *I don't even know what I'm doing.* Last Friday, I would've asked him about three things under my floorboard, but now I have this urgent desire to make things right. Also, if Carmen isn't my secret admirer, it seems more likely that Pete is.

When I turn the corner toward Pete's locker, my stomach drops. He's surrounded by a crowd of people—other basketball players and girls with perfect blowouts I don't recognize. *This is why you should always plan things,* I scold myself.

I'm about to turn around when he spots me above a brunette girl's head. He raises his hand immediately and waves.

I give him a small wave back, and that's all he needs. He excuses himself from the group and walks over to me.

"Hey!" he says with a wide smile when he reaches me. "I didn't see you at the game the other night. You said you wanted to talk afterward. . . ."

"Yeah," I mutter, still ashamed from what Carmen told me. "I'm really sorry about that."

"No worries. Hey, where are you headed? I'll walk with you."

"My locker."

"Great." He smiles widely again. I wonder if he realizes this wasn't the way to my locker at all. I feel my cheeks redden and

I turn back around the same way I came. He follows, not once looking back at the group he left behind. It reminds me of why I felt so special being his girlfriend—when he's with you, all his focus is on you, like nothing else matters.

"How's basketball going?" I ask, realizing how easy it is to fall back into conversation with someone you know.

"It's going great. We won on Friday. Now we have a bye week until playoffs."

"That's huge," I say.

"Yeah," he continues. "So since I don't have a game this Friday, I was thinking of going to the Hudson Valley Orchard for hot apple cider and donuts. My sister has been talking about it nonstop."

"Oh yeah. I love it there in the winter."

Barns aren't normally my thing, even though my town has a ton of them. They smell like rotting hay in the thick of summertime and are overcrowded with tourists picking apples in the fall. But in the winter, people in town go for the live music and food.

"Would you want to go with me?" he asks quickly. It catches me off guard. Last year we never went on a real date. The most we did was hang out with Carmen and other guys from his team. There was that one time we went to the movies when his mom dropped us off and it almost felt like a real date until mine picked us up again. Pete always talked about where he'd want to take me when he could finally drive us places, but his birthday is in May, so we never got the chance. Now he drives a black Audi, and when girls from the bus see it pulling up into the parking lot, they pull down the windows to wave at him. Plenty of them would love to go on a date with Pete. Why doesn't he ask one of them?

I look up at him and he meets my eyes, anxiously awaiting my answer. Maybe one-on-one time is long overdue. *I thought you were in love,* I remember Sydney saying as she did my nails.

"Sure," I say as we reach my locker. "What time?"

"How about seven? I can pick you up."

I nod. "Sounds great."

"Good," he says, smiling. "Well, I have to get to class. Mrs. D said if I'm late one more time she'll tell my coach. But I'm looking forward to Friday."

"Me too."

He smiles again and I stare at him in amazement as he walks away. What just happened? The last thing I expected was for him to ask me out on a date.

I turn to my locker and fiddle with the lock. Eventually, I get the numbers right and when I open the door, I can't believe my luck.

There's another paper heart.

I used to think people who gasp were faking it. But I gasp on the spot.

I clutch the paper heart to my real one before opening it.

"Whoa, watercolors! I wish I'd thought of that!" a voice says behind me. I spin around and it's Sarah Chang.

"Me too," I say as she starts digging in her tote bag. She must have paper hearts for me.

"But I'm sure the ones in here are equally impressive in their own right. You have a bunch more paper hearts—hold on."

Soon she pulls out a small stack, and as I accept them, I put the watercolored one on top so it doesn't get lost in the pile.

I'm curious about whether she's received my paper heart yet, but I can't exactly ask without giving myself away. "So what made you switch from treasurer to planning committee this year?" I ask instead.

Her eyes search me for a second, like she's wondering why I'm talking to her. "To be honest, I spent the first three years of high school pretending I could avoid it." She shrugs. "So, I made it a goal of mine to actually participate in school functions this year. You know, get the whole experience in before it's over. I figured if I was going to do that, I might as well make it fun."

For a second, I wonder if she's going to ask me why I quit, but she doesn't. She must be too polite for that—just another reason to feel bad that my friends were mean to her.

"How many more hearts do you have to pass out? Do you need help?"

She shakes her head. "Normally, I play Roblox in between periods. This is giving me something better to do."

"Well, not if you were playing Rockefeller Street."

"I mean, *obviously* that's my game of choice." She laughs. "But I can sacrifice some Roblox time for this. I actually enjoy seeing people's faces when I hand them paper hearts. It's like I'm Santa with my tote bag."

"Or Cupid," I say.

"Yeah, that would make a lot more sense, wouldn't it?"

I notice her tote bag is different from the last one I saw. This one says GUAC IS EXTRA BUT SO ARE YOU. I'm about to ask her where it's from because I like it so much, when I see her looking around like she's worried who might see us together.

"Well, this Cupid is off to make more end games happen. See you around."

"Oh, okay . . . bye," I say, stuffing the paper hearts in my backpack.

All but my watercolored paper heart.

Chapter 12

"I CAN'T BELIEVE YOU'RE GOING ON A DATE WITH PETE!" Carmen squeals louder than the time she did when he wrote *Love, Pete* on my birthday card. I thought things might be awkward between us after the ride to school this morning, but I was so wrong. Not when I have the kind of gossip that she's been waiting for. We're in her car, and she's hanging on my every word.

"Let's not make a big deal of this. It's just a date. . . ." I trail off.

"Too late," she says. "This is a very big deal. I *knew* he'd want you back. You guys are perfect for each other."

"I don't know about that," I say. "I did break up with him last year, after all. But it feels like it can be different this time."

She looks at me. "What does that mean?"

"I don't know. He just seems *changed*."

"Changed how?" Carmen asks, eyeing me.

"I don't know exactly. I guess I'm just excited we're going out on Friday. We never used to do that sort of thing."

She nods. "He's definitely trying to impress you. This is good."

I realize I'm leaving out the whole paper hearts part. That's what makes him the most different—if it's him. It could still very well be Carmen, but either way I'm keeping my mouth shut as we continue to drive. She's taking me to the library to drop my book off before heading home.

The last paper heart is still on my mind. *See a castle from a view as beautiful as you.* I've been thinking about what it could mean all day and I still have no idea. There's also a number 6 underneath . . . or maybe it's a 9.

I want to check the paper heart again, but I feel guilty even thinking about this now. I haven't been able to forget what Carmen said to me about being a bad friend. In a way, it's almost as haunting as the accident itself. Can you truly apologize for your behavior if you don't remember it?

"So how are things with Anthony?" I ask.

She keeps her eyes on the road. A small smile escapes her lips. "Perfect."

The rest of the ride I happily talk about Anthony and Carmen instead of me and Pete. She completely gushes about Anthony, and Carmen *never* gushes. In fact, I'm normally the one with a crush, and she's the one who finds something wrong with pretty much everybody. Tons of boys have liked her, but she always has some excuse: *Too short. Gross.* Or, if they're neither of those things: *he seems like he likes me a little too much, you know?* And the truth is no, I don't.

Sometimes I think she gets these phrases from her mom. I'll always remember when Carmen found out her parents were getting divorced at the end of sixth grade. One day her dad just got up and left them. Carmen was devastated. To be honest, I don't know if she ever got over it.

Now Carmen's always trying to help her mom find the right guys. She goes through her mom's online profile. She says that even the ones who look good online end up being total duds on the actual date, which is a shame because I love her mom and she deserves the best man ever. Sometimes I wonder if she's just afraid of getting hurt, though, and writes people off. Carmen used to tell me stories of how she'd hear her mom crying at night, but when she asked her, she'd deny it. Carmen's like that too. When she's upset, she keeps it all bottled up. The only way I can ever tell something is going on is when her face gives her away. Just like her eyes give it away when she's lying, her lips give it away when she's upset. She presses them together like she did earlier, so tight it's like she's trying to press all the emotion out of her.

When people ask about my accident in front of her or talk about the dance, it looks like she has no lips at all. At least her expressions make it obvious. People shut up immediately. One time when I was binge-watching *Law & Order*, I decided that Carmen would make a good interrogator.

But the way Carmen's looking right now makes me happy.

I can see in her eyes that she's genuinely happy. I've known Anthony since middle school. I know that he laughs at his own jokes and that he always gives the wrong answer when he's called on in calculus, and sometimes after gym class the amount of Axe he puts on makes me dizzy. But Carmen knows these things too, and if she still thinks he's perfect, I'm thrilled for her.

She tells me how they sat next to each other at the diner after the game. How he finally kissed her when they got outside. How she can't wait until they kiss again. Her excitement is contagious—I want to want someone like that. The memory of Sydney telling me I was in love pops into my mind. *Maybe you did feel that way before.*

When we finally park at the library, Carmen checks her phone immediately. There's already a new text from Anthony. Whatever it says makes Carmen smile. She starts replying instantly. Apparently, they're already over the playing-hard-to-get stage.

I laugh. "You can stay here. I'll be quick."

"Sounds good," she says without even looking up from her phone.

I slide out of the car and make my way to the library, with *Pride and Prejudice* in my bag. But once I'm inside, I see Sarah at the front desk, not Andy. I linger at the doorway for a second with a feeling I can't explain. Am I *disappointed*? Andy must be growing on me.

Sarah's smile is wide as she helps an elderly lady check out.

When she's done, she looks up and sees me at the doorway. I awkwardly wave, and as she waves back I wonder if she got my heart yet—until Andy suddenly pops out from behind a stack of books, a dimpled grin on his face.

"I knew you'd come by to see me," he says with a wink.

"Yes, this has nothing to do with the fact that I finished my library book," I deadpan.

"Well, you read this very quickly," he says as we walk toward the drop-off bin. "Either you're a super-quick reader or you were dying to see me."

"I *am* a fast reader, thank you very much," I say as we reach the bin. I open my backpack. Normally, I'm the girl who is organized to the max. I color-code my binders and secretly keep my textbooks in alphabetical order. But my backpack might be as messy as my life right now. I dig inside, searching for the book among all my binders and folders for school. Once I pull it out, the loose paper heart underneath falls out. I reach for the heart, but it's too late.

"Still chasing paper hearts, I see," Andy says, picking it up before I can.

There's no point lying now.

"Yeah. I'm stuck on this one, though," I admit. "I have no idea what it means."

He looks at me, and for a second I hope he asks to help again. But he doesn't.

"So you still have no idea who's sending these?"

I drop the book in the bin with a heavy *thud.* "Sorry. I didn't mean to be that loud."

"Don't try to get out of this question," he says, grinning again. "You *do* have a theory, don't you?"

I do, and I feel my cheeks get warm as I think about Pete.

"There's one person I think it could be. But I'll have a better idea on Friday."

"Mysterious answer. Why on Friday?" he asks.

"Because we're going out on a date."

He looks down at his feet and then back up at me. "A date? Who's the lucky guy?"

"His name is Pete," I answer honestly. It's not like we go to the same school, so his name won't mean anything.

Andy squints at me. "And why do you think your mystery admirer is basketball star Pete Yearling?"

Welp. I guess I was wrong about him not knowing who Pete is.

"Well, for starters, he's my ex-boyfriend—" I begin, but he stops me.

"Why would an *ex-boyfriend* be sending you letters? I'm not a cook, but getting back with an ex is like reheating a soufflé, don't you think?"

Even though his words have a hint of humor to them, there's irritation in his eyes—but I'm irritated too.

"No." I cross my arms. "If he's been sending me these hearts, it's *romantic.*"

"I don't know." He shakes his head hard. He isn't just disagreeing with me—it's like he's trying to wipe the idea of me going on a date with someone else out of his mind. "Are you going to ask Pete if it's him?"

"I don't want to ruin the surprise. I'm just going to see if he drops any hints."

He grimaces. "Seems like you have become a detective after all. I get why you kicked me off the case now."

It isn't what he says but the way he says it that makes my heart drop. He seems . . . *sad?* Maybe he's just thinking about the girl that broke his heart again.

"Can I ask you another question?" he asks.

I nod.

"Do you want it to be him?"

I blink. "What kind of a question is that?" I ask.

He grins. "An easy one, if you know the answer."

I'm about to argue that he's being a jerk—that everything may appear simple to him from the outside but there's more to it. But then I hear my name from across the room. It's not exactly a library voice either.

I whip my head around to see Carmen in the doorway. Everyone else spins around too. Carmen mouths the word *sorry* to everyone before waving her hand for me to come.

I turn back to Andy, whose sadness has disappeared. He keeps his eyes on me instead of scolding Carmen.

"I should go," I say.

"I think the whole library knows that. I'll see you around."

I smile as if to thank him for not making a big deal about Carmen's lack of awareness, but I'm actually relieved that Carmen came when she did. Do I want my mystery admirer to be Pete? Seriously, how am I supposed to answer that? This isn't some silly scavenger hunt; it's a way to fill in the blanks. My chance to remember.

But Andy doesn't know that. He doesn't know a lot of things. *Because you haven't told him,* I remind myself.

As I join Carmen, she gives me a look that says *what was taking so long?* But she must still be mildly embarrassed about the whole library looking at her, because we walk out together in silence. The second we're outside and can finally talk again, she blurts out, "Was that nerd bothering you?"

It takes me a second to realize she's talking about Andy.

"No. His name is Andy," I say, correcting her. "He works there."

"Andy?" she repeats. There's a long pause like she's waiting for me to say something. "You're way too nice to guys sometimes. It's not like you're a walking charity case."

I force a smile. There's no point in explaining to her that Andy's more than some guy I just met. It would only make her angry to know he's who I was with the night I ditched the game. Maybe that's why instead I say what she wants to hear.

"So, what should I wear on Friday?"

She smiles instantly. It's only as she starts rambling on about possibilities that I realize Andy still has my last paper heart.

~

Later that night when I'm lying in bed, I message Andy.

You still have my paper heart.

He responds with a phone number so I text it with the same message.

You still have my paper heart.

He sends me a crying laugh emoji and then an actual response.

I'll give it back after your date on Friday.

Um . . . why?

Why not?

I groan. Why is he being difficult?

Just forget him. It's not like I really need Andy, I tell myself. I already memorized the clue: *See a castle from a view as beautiful as you.* The only thing I can't remember is if the number underneath is a 6 or a 9. Or 16 or 19. Okay, maybe I do need that heart.

I type back.

Seriously?

A few seconds go by that feel like forever until he responds.

Let's make a deal. If you wait until after Friday, I'll help
you solve this one. You said you haven't solved it, right?
And I bet I can help . . .

He's so infuriating, especially when he's right.

Deal

~

But even though I make this deal, I can't get the next paper heart out of my mind. Later that night when I'm alone in bed with Wi-Fi, I google what I wanted to hours ago: *Castles near Poughkeepsie.*

I'm hoping that more than a White Castle shows up—I doubt my admirer would send me to a burger joint, but what other castles could they be talking about in the Hudson Valley? I'm shocked, however, to find a whole list of them. The first article on my screen is *13 Magnificent Castles in Upstate New York Straight Out of a Fairy Tale.*

My jaw drops. Thirteen? At this rate, I'll never find out who my secret admirer is.

But it needs to be a castle from a beautiful view, I remind myself. As I scan the list, there's one in particular that jumps out to me, in Beacon, a couple of towns over. Well, sort of in Beacon. It's a castle on an island in the Hudson River that you can *see* from Beacon. Bingo. From there, I'm on a roll. All I do is google *How to see Bannerman Castle in Beacon* and up pops a link to Breakneck Ridge, a hiking trail along the river that brings you to an overlook. *A beautiful view.*

Who needs Andy or his fun facts when you have Google? I think smugly as I shut my laptop.

Chapter 13

EVEN THOUGH I MADE A DEAL WITH ANDY THAT I'D WAIT, I can't get Bannerman Castle out of my mind. I have two options. One, wait for Andy like I said I would, or two, find a new way to Bannerman without him. By lunchtime the next day I have an idea: I'm going to rally the troops like old times.

"Who's up for an afterschool hike?" I say once everyone takes the first bite of their salad.

Carmen raises her eyebrow. *"Hike?"*

I'm not sure if she's surprised I want to do something or just against hiking in general. Maybe both. I'll have to lay it on thick.

"Yes, there's this hiking trail called Breakneck that is supposed to be *a blast*," I say. "There's a loop that goes all the way up the mountain. It's supposed to be pretty challenging."

I look across the table to see nothing but blank faces. So I try my last resort.

"We could get really cool photos from the top."

"I'm in!" Carmen says. Jess and Katie quickly nod too.

"Great. Today?" I suggest, everything falling perfectly into place.

But then Carmen shakes her head. "I'm hanging out with Anthony tonight."

I forgot that Carmen's mom lets her do stuff that late on a school night. My parents would never.

"Well, what if we go right after school?" I ask. "Anthony has basketball practice anyways, so you can't hang out with him until later."

"I'm free," Katie offers.

I turn to Jess. "Same," she says.

Carmen crosses her arms. "I'm not saying I don't want to go—just not today. I don't even have hiking gear."

"Wear your gym clothes—that's what I was planning on doing. Don't you have those Lululemon leggings in your locker? And then after we go you can tell Anthony how much fun you had while he was at practice."

She studies my face like she's searching for the real reason I want to go so badly, but I just give her a smile that says *pretty please?*

"Fine," she says, uncrossing her arms. "Meet at my car after school."

And just like that, I rally the troops.

~

"So is this trail called Breakneck because you can actually break your neck?" Jess asks on our hike up the mountain. "Because I'm not trying to do that."

"It *is* high up," Katie says. At first, I'm worried she's going to suggest not going all the way to the ridge, but she squeals, "The pictures are going to be amazing!"

"Yeah, they will." Carmen smiles. Her hair is in a perfect topknot, ready for a photo op.

"You guys are ridiculous," I say.

"We're ridiculous?" Carmen retorts. "This is the first time you've wanted to do anything *in forever.*"

"Well, I'm here, aren't I?" I ask. but as I say it a part of me feels guilty because I have an ulterior motive.

Carmen doesn't notice. "You are! And I love it!" Carmen shouts right there in the middle of the woods. Then she laughs loudly in my direction. "It's good to get out. It'll give you practice for your date with Pete on Friday.

"Carmen," Katie hisses.

"What? I can shout," Carmen says, brushing her off. Then there's a mischievous look on her face that makes me know she's going to yell even louder. "I love my friends!!!" she roars.

The four of us laugh and keep on hiking up the mountain. There's nothing but bare trees and fallen pinecones along the trail. Luckily, the snow from the other week has melted, so we're able to make it up the steep trail. It's hard—way harder than I expected it to be—but we still manage to talk on our way up.

At first, we joke about the funniest paper hearts we have received. Katie received the best one from a guy in her Latin class. It said *I think we've had our eye on each other all year— Carpe DM me sometime.* I give him points for creativity. It's definitely something Andy would say. I almost tell my friends about him, but then I hold back. How do I tell them about Andy without disclosing the paper hearts? Suddenly I feel guilty for keeping this from my friends. Since when do I keep things from them?

"Hey, Ella. You okay?" Carmen asks as I stop walking.

"Yeah . . . I'm . . . just a little out of breath."

"Girl, me too," Jess says, passing me. "These views better be worth it."

I take a deep breath and start walking again. It wasn't the truth, but by the time we're nearing the top, I'm actually breathing heavily. There's nothing like a tough hike to remind me I really should have exercised more this year. My body wants to collapse right there on the trail. I step on a branch, making a loud *crunch* that snaps me out of it.

"We made it!" Carmen cheers as she spots the overlook up ahead. The view is as spectacular as the pictures.

I suck in a deep breath of the pine-scented air, catching up to her to search for my next paper heart. I can't let her or any of my friends find the paper heart before me. How on earth would I explain that?" But once the trail levels out and I'm about to move toward the ridge, Carmen grabs my hand.

"Selfie!" she says, reaching her arm out as far as it goes to get the view in the background.

"Ugh, never mind," she says, dropping her iPhone. "We need to get closer."

"Good idea," I say, rushing ahead of her.

"Let's figure out the best angle," I suggest. My friends nod, and as they start looking through their iPhone lenses for the best view, I pretend to do the same but really, I'm searching the ground for a watercolored heart. I beeline for the patch of grass in front of the view of the castle—but there's nothing on the ground.

"Oooh, what is that?" Katie asks behind me.

My heart drops. Oh no.

I turn to see her staring right at me. *Oh no,* I think, but when I look at her hand, she's not holding a paper heart.

"What?" I ask.

"Behind you," she says. "Is that a castle?"

"Oh yeah," I say. "Bannerman Castle. I saw online that it was built on the island in the Revolutionary War or something."

"So awesome!" Carmen says. "We have to take a picture in front of *that*."

Carmen finds a rock in front of me and sets the self-timer on her phone, before the three of them quickly huddle around me and smile before the flash goes off.

Even as we take the photo, I'm scanning the ground. I was sure this was where the next paper heart would be. What am I missing? After the group photo I suggest that everyone takes individual shots while we are here and my friends happily oblige—but really, I just want more time to search for the next message.

What did the last paper heart say? Six or nine? Gah, neither of those numbers make any sense, I think as I'm investigating a nearby tree. Maybe there will be a paper heart hanging from one of the branches?

"You're up, Ella," Jess says. I look from the pine needles to her.

"For what?"

"Pictures, *duh*."

"Oh . . . I don't need one with just me." I shift and a branch snaps beneath my feet.

"No way!" Carmen says. "You need a new picture so you

can start posting again. It's getting ridiculous how off the grid you are when you look this good."

"Er . . . thanks," I say, reluctantly moving from the tree to the edge. I suddenly fear that the paper heart has blown away. Maybe that's why I can't find it.

No. I shake my head. *Whoever your admirer is, is making sure these hearts get to you,* I think, remembering how the last one was tied securely to a ribbon and how the ones before that were hand delivered to me. It was safe to say that there wasn't a paper heart here.

I sigh. How did I get the clue so wrong? Am I misremembering what it said? I could have sworn it said to look for a castle from a beautiful view. Where else could that be?

Once I'm standing in front of the castle in the distance, I smile for the photo but on the inside, I feel nothing but disappointment.

~

The rest of the week my thoughts shift from wondering what the paper heart means, to anxiously thinking about what my date on Friday with Pete will be like. I hope there will be butterflies to replace the current feeling in my stomach. But I can't help thinking about what Andy asked me . . . *do I want my admirer to be Pete?*

Finally, it's Friday night. I change into a red shirt that ties at the waist, dark-washed skinny jeans, and black booties. Normally, Ashley and I have completely opposite styles but she has this bomber jacket that has way more of a cool date vibe than any of my peacoats, so I sneak into her room to borrow it.

I don't know why I'm so nervous. I've hung out with Pete before and everything, but there's something about going on an actual date with him that feels more mature somehow. It's ironic how doing adult things sometimes can have a way of making you feel like a complete baby.

But I know deep down I'm anxious for other reasons. I'm expecting that it'll give me some clarity once and for all if Pete's my admirer. In my mind, all signs point to Pete. But like Andy pointed out, my heart still doesn't know what it wants, so I'm also hoping this date changes that.

Pete arrives a few minutes late, which I'm actually grateful for despite how punctual I normally am. I had finished getting ready about a half hour ago out of nerves and am doing last-minute touch-ups to my makeup when the doorbell rings. I bolt out of bed and throw Ashley's bomber jacket on, suddenly hoping I don't run into her. I didn't exactly ask to borrow it.

As I make my way downstairs, my heart stops. Dad is at the bottom of the stairs talking to someone. My first thought is Ashley, but then I see the front door is already open. Pete's inside.

Oh no.

I had told my dad I was going to the Hudson Valley Orchard but I didn't exactly tell him it was for a *date.* Or that it was with Pete. Not because it was going to be an issue. My dad loves Pete. Last year when we started hanging out, he called him a *standup guy from a great family*. In movies dads are typically seen grilling their daughters' boyfriends—threatening to kill them if they hurt them. That would never be my dad. He's way too cool for that.

As I begin walking down the stairs, I hear the two of them laughing about God knows what.

"Hey, Ella," my dad says when he sees me. "Pete was just telling me there was going to be fried dough at the orchard. I was telling him about your first fried dough experience."

The time I put so much powder on mine I walked around with a white beard the entire day, with pictures to prove it.

"If you're going to tell embarrassing stories, at least let me be in the room," I say, forcing a smile. Suddenly, I wish he were grilling Pete instead.

My dad looks at me and tilts his head a little. I wonder if it's because I have more makeup on than usual, but he doesn't say anything.

"Oh no, I really enjoyed it," Pete says, stepping in. "I'm hoping there will be a repeat later."

"I will *not* be having a fried dough beard tonight."

"Okay, but you will be home by eleven," my dad says, looking from me to Pete.

Pete nods. "Sure thing. It was great seeing you, Mr. Fitzpatrick."

I can't help but think it's something a standup guy from a great family would say. Maybe that's why my dad is smiling so big right now. Or maybe it's because his loner daughter as of late is actually going out on a Friday night.

"Okay, bye Dad," I say before he can tell another story. Pete follows me as I scurry out, the door shutting behind us.

"Let me help you down—these stairs are a little icy," he says before we walk down the steps with my arm looped in his. It feels natural and makes my anxieties disappear.

Maybe going out with a standup guy won't be a bad thing at all.

~

Just when I think a first date couldn't be any more romantic, it starts to snow as we get to the orchard. Not too heavy that we have to go home or anything. The perfect amount of snow that you can see falling but light enough that you barely feel anything when it touches you. When the first snowflake falls on my cheek, I can't help but beam. Waiting for snow must be kind of like waiting for love. If it happened all the time, it wouldn't be as exciting, but when it finally comes, it's magical.

"What're you smiling about?" Pete asks, leading me toward

the barn. We can hear the music buzzing behind the shut doors.

"It's snowing!" I say. "I just love when it snows like this."

"I planned that for you too," he jokes.

"Perfect snow. Check," I say, looking at my pretend clipboard. "What's next on the agenda?"

"Well, after your dad's story, I know we have to hit up the fried dough station. But let's save dessert for last. First, we should get hot chocolate and roam the gift vendors. I still have to get something for my mom for Valentine's Day."

There's plenty of sweet things I remember him doing. Volunteering at a youth clinic over the summer for underprivileged kids. Making sure to be a good big brother to his younger sister. But I guess there's small stuff you can miss even after almost a year of dating.

"Aw. Do you always get your mom a gift for Valentine's Day?"

"Yeah, usually I buy her flowers, but since we're here, I figured you can help me. You're a girl and all—I'm assuming she'll like something you choose."

I smile. "That's so sweet of you. I'd be happy to help."

But as we walk over to the hot chocolate line, it takes everything in me to keep my cool. If Pete gets his mom a valentine every year, he really might be my mystery admirer after all. I already knew he was thoughtful, but this proves it yet again.

Then there's another part of me that wants to push this thought out of my head. This is my first real date. I shouldn't be trying to find out if he's my paper-hearts admirer now. Why am I even thinking about that? I should be enjoying Pete's company.

The snow is still falling so gently, like it's just kissing the ground. It makes me wonder if Pete will try to kiss me when he walks me to my doorstep tonight.

Pete smiles and then grabs my hand again as he leads me inside the barn and then to the hot chocolate line.

We stand in line and I think about telling him about the Hot Chocolate Theory, but then get mad at myself for indirectly thinking about Andy again.

Suddenly, we are first in line. I reach for my wallet, but he pays for two hot chocolates. When he hands me mine, my heart melts like the marshmallows floating on top.

"Thanks," I say. *For the hot chocolate, and the paper hearts,* I think.

With his free hand, he grabs mine and we begin walking again.

And I can't help but think that maybe we hold hands because it's the closest thing we can do to hold on to the moment. In a second, all the good memories come back to me like they never left. Dancing at homecoming together and not caring that everyone was watching. Cheering at his basketball games from the bleachers with his number that Carmen painted on my cheek. Finding him waiting by my locker in between classes to surprise me. Walking to the coffee shop during our free period even though he didn't like coffee—he said he just wanted to be with me. At the time, I just wanted to be with him too. What happened?

"Is everything okay?" he asks, releasing my hand. "I'm sorry, I didn't mean to rush you."

I shake my head. "No, it's not you. I just . . . I just struggle being with you without thinking about *before*." I pause and look him in the eye. "I just wish there was a way to take back the weeks I lost," I say, directly quoting the first message from my admirer. "You know, to figure out what I was thinking."

I hope to gauge some sort of reaction from Pete, but all he does is blink and he does it so fast, I don't know if it's because of what I said. I sigh.

"Look, El. I know that feeling. I mean, do you believe I don't think about us every time I see you at school? I tried to get over you, but when you reached out and said you wanted to talk . . . I just felt like maybe after everything, I could give us a second chance like you wanted after the accident," he reminds me.

I feel myself blush at the memory. I remember asking for him back, like it would be simple. But it wasn't simple then and it isn't now either. His eyes are different this time, though— they look hopeful.

My eyes widen.

"Shoot. I've already said too much," he says quickly. "What

I'm trying to say is that we had great memories but I want to make new ones. So let's not think about the past or anything tonight. Let's stay in the moment and have a great real date like we always talked about."

He smiles at me now. I don't know what to say, so I take his hand back and his smile becomes even bigger.

Pete leads me to an open bench by the live band playing old 90s country music. There's a crowd forming around them but we stay off to the side, not really paying attention to the music. I think Pete may be nervous about having a great real date as much as I am because he starts rambling off stories—stories, I realize by the third one, that I'm not a part of because I've been MIA this year, missing every single senior prank and skip day. But Pete's a great storyteller. He waves his arms in excitement and sets the scene so you feel like you're there. I sip my hot chocolate, listening to him.

Carmen has been telling me I've been missing everything for months now, but for the first time, it really hits. I didn't just lose those eleven weeks. I've lost more. I've lost my senior year from recovering and feeling sorry for myself because for the first time, my life wasn't perfect. But maybe the fact that I even felt that way is the saddest part of all.

Once we finish our hot chocolate, we wander around the local vendors for gifts. I'm tempted to drop more hints about the paper hearts, but I try to listen to Pete and stay in the moment.

"What about this?" Pete asks, holding up a picture frame made of pieces of glass in different shades of pink. "I can tell her to save it for the photo we take together at Senior Day."

"That's perfect," I say. "She'll love it."

"You think so?"

"Definitely. You'll win Son of the Year," I say, forcing a smile before Pete heads to the cashier. Student government doesn't have a Senior Day with parents, but there's always a small party for the graduating class at the end of the year that the planning committee throws. We would make photo albums with all the memorable moments. It took hours of cutting and pasting on top of finding the best pictures, but it was always worth it in the end to see how happy the graduating seniors were. It suddenly dawns on me that nobody will be making one for me.

You had to quit, I remind myself.

On the first day of school this year, there was an informational meeting for everyone who wanted to join student government, as always. When I arrived, only two sophomore girls had gotten to the classroom before me. They were chatting as two best friends might when they think nobody else is around, and they didn't stop because they didn't see me at the doorway.

One of them jokingly asked if the other thought I'd be as much of a dictator this year or if a bump to the head knocked some niceness into me.

Everything about what she said was hypocritical—she wasn't exactly being nice talking about me behind my back.

It was also a little too soon to be making fun of my accident, if you asked me. The old me would've probably called her out right then and there. The new me was struggling, though. When people used to stare at me in the hall, I knew it was for one of two reasons. Either they thought I was pretty, or they wanted to see who was lucky enough to date Pete Yearling. On that first day of school, all I could do was wonder what people were thinking. My accident was old news, and it wasn't like people could see the scars underneath my perfect first-day outfit, although I was still constantly tugging at my sleeves.

As if I wasn't self-conscious enough, I couldn't help but think about the get-well cards—the ones that made me realize what people actually thought of me.

As these girls laughed at me in the student government room, I remembered the fake letters they had sent me hoping to see me back at school soon. The thought made me nauseous.

So, I backed away from the classroom door without looking back.

When I got home my mom raised her eyebrows and asked why I was back so early. I told her that I wasn't doing student government this year but left out what I had overheard. I think when she was examining my face, though, she detected a sadness. That's why over the next couple of weeks she would ask if I had changed my mind. I hadn't, and the fact that she kept bringing it up was only making it worse. I suddenly realized what it must feel like to be Ashley—before she picked up the guitar, my mom was always insisting that she join a club after school. Maybe that's why by the hundredth time my mom asked if I was considering rejoining student government, Ashley stood up for me, telling her no and to leave me alone. In that moment, I had an appreciation for her in a way I hadn't in a long time. It was a moment that reminded me that despite our differences, we have each other's backs.

But thinking about Senior Day now, a part of me wonders if my mom was right. Should I have just tried to stick with it instead of feeling sorry for myself? Maybe that's really what my admirer is trying to tell me. Is that why they're sending me on all these adventures? So I can actually do things again and live my life?

Well, if that's the case, they're right.

I watch Pete receive the paper bag with the frame wrapped inside.

"Ready?" Pete asks once he turns around.

"Ready," I answer . . . and I mean it in more than one way.

~

As Pete drives me home, I wonder again if he's going to kiss me.

We had such a great night. I reach into my gift bag and find the paperweight I purchased for my dad. It's in the shape of an actual human heart—so realistic you can see all the veins and other parts of the heart—the aorta, the pulmonary valve, and more that I know, thanks to my dad being a science professor. This is the type of Valentine's Day present he'll appreciate.

My fingers trail over the paper weight in the same path the blood takes. People think the heart is on the left side of the body because that's where you can feel the left ventricle pumping blood to the lungs. But it's really in the middle. I'm sure there's some scientific reason for that but my theory is because our hearts are at the center of everything we do.

"I'm so happy you found that," Pete says. I look over and his eyes are on me. I wonder how long he has been watching. "My mom's going to love her gift too."

"She will. She's lucky to have such a thoughtful son."

Pete smiles. "It's the least I could do. She brought me into this world."

It's like everything that comes out of his mouth is so impossibly nice. Every second that goes by, the surer I am that my mystery admirer is Pete. It has to be someone caring to go through so much trouble.

After we picked out our gifts, we found the fried dough station, and he told me stories about his teammates and family members. He even told me an embarrassing story about himself when he was younger to even out the score since my dad had already told him one of mine. It was beyond endearing—

just like all of the paper hearts have been. *It just has to be him,* I think as we reach my driveway.

"I'll walk you to your door," he says once we're parked.

The snow is still falling, enough of it sticking to the driveway so that our shoes make footprints as we walk.

When we make it to the steps, I just put one bootie on the wood, forgetting all about the ice underneath the fallen snow. I lose my balance just a little, but Pete's there to steady me.

"Sorry—I should've reminded you it's icy," he says, holding my arms. I can't believe he's apologizing to me when I'm the one being a klutz. Before I can say anything, we're at my doorstep. "I hope this was the first date you imagined," he says. I nod. Then he bends down and kisses me.

My lips remember his. They feel so warm now compared to the cold air, and I press harder. It's only for a few seconds, though. Soon he pulls away. He's probably too much of a gentleman to kiss me deeply with my dad right inside, but I would've liked to see if a real kiss with Pete would give me butterflies. When he pulls back, he smiles widely before walking down the steps.

"Good night, Ella."

"Good night," I say, smiling back. And just like that my first real date is over.

Spinning around, I find the key in my pocket and let myself into my warm home. Once I'm inside, I remove my gloves and then check my phone. I didn't have the urge to check it once on our date. But the smile still on my face quickly disappears when I see a string of texts from Andy.

Did you figure out your next paper heart yet? If not, I can help.

I hope that last text didn't sound patronizing. I'm a #feminist.

OK. There's no way this date of yours is taking this long. This guy does not look like he has anything interesting to say.

I text back immediately.

How do you know if he looks interesting???

In seconds I see three dots and then a new message appears.

Maybe I looked him up in our library system and saw his picture on his library card . . .

I laugh and type back one word.

Stalker.

His rebuttal is fast.

Excuse me. I thought after all these paper hearts, you were into this sort of thing.

164

It makes me laugh.

If you imply the paper hearts are creepy again, you won't
get to go on the next adventure with me.

I wait for him to reply right away like he has been doing, but he doesn't. Maybe I was too harsh? Whatever, it's true. He thinks he knows everything. My conversations with Pete *were* interesting. I enjoyed hearing his stories—or at least I thought I did. Why am I letting Andy make me doubt myself? Contrary to what he may believe with Hot Chocolate Theory and all, I'm not the kind of girl who just wants the romance. I do want love. I just haven't found it yet. I groan and head upstairs.

When I get to my bedroom, I crouch down on the floor, peeling back the fuzzy rug next to the bed to my secret hideaway.

The hot chocolates Pete and I drank had those paper sleeves wrapped around them. I had discretely snuck mine into my purse when Pete wasn't looking before we threw our empty cups out in the recycling bin.

I open the floorboard now to put my first-date sleeve inside. It's been a while since I've had anything new to add.

Out of habit, I look at my three mystery items. The flower, the Polaroid photo, and the key. Something about seeing my smile in the Polaroid makes me sigh. I so want to be that happy again. Why couldn't I just figure out what this all means?

I flip the photo over in my hands and see the handwriting scrawled on the back.

NYC 2/8

I have a flashback to the last time I was in the city. Not the time on 2/8—I don't remember that—but the time before, when I went to see a Broadway play with Ashley and my mom. It was right after the holidays, and there were snowcapped towers, and lights shining in every window.

Suddenly, I think back to the paper heart I haven't been able to solve. *See a castle from a view as beautiful as you.* Could the castle be in New York City?

I whip out my phone and google castles in Manhattan. The first thing that comes up is a place called Belvedere Castle. It's in the middle of Central Park.

I start scrolling through all the images on Google until I see the lamppost outside the stone walls. I zoom in, my hand shaking excitedly. It's the same one from the Polaroid. Just when I don't think my heart can beat any faster, I hear a knock on my door.

"Just a second!" I say, scrambling to shove the photo and everything else under the floorboard and throwing the rug back over it. "Come in," I say once I'm sitting on my bed.

My mom pops her head in. "Just wanted to say good night. How'd the date go? We missed Pete."

"Great," I say, my heart still beating fast.

"Okay, okay, we don't need to talk about it. Good night."

"Good night."

When the door shuts behind her, I let out a sigh of relief. That was close. But not as close as I feel to answers. I look at my items again, this time seeing them in a new light.

The rose must be from the florist I went to after the first paper heart. The photo was taken at Belvedere Castle. Now I just need to figure out the key—it must lead to something important. I take my key chain out of my purse. I haven't driven in almost a year but I still carry it around because other important things are on it like my school ID and the keys to my house. I slide the new key onto my chain—maybe one day soon I'll know what it's for.

I pull out my phone to look at pictures of the castle again when I see a new text from Andy.

Please forgive me. I'd really like to go on this adventure with you.

"I'm going tomorrow," I type back. *And I need to know that number now,* I think.

When? Does this mean you solved it?

Yes. 9 AM

I see the three dots appear and then his reply.

It's a date.

I know he's just teasing, so I send a joking text right back.

       I can't date you Sherlock. I'm a professional.

As long as that's your only excuse.

I don't know if it was meant to be as flirty as it seems, but I can't help blushing before I type back.

       See you tomorrow and bring that paper heart.

Chapter 14

"WHY CAN'T YOU JUST DOWNLOAD YOUR TICKET LIKE everyone else?"

Andy and I have just arrived at the train station and he insists on purchasing a physical copy. He starts pressing the buttons on the screen.

"I thought you'd appreciate old-school, Miss Paper Hearts Girl."

"That's different," I say. "*This* is a waste of time. We could be on the train already."

"Go check the track, will ya?" he says, smiling. "You're making me anxious."

"Fine," I say, leaving him as he reaches for his wallet.

The train station is normally busy on weekends and today is not an exception. I zigzag through a Girl Scout troop and a large family wearing matching New York Knicks beanies.

When I make it to the screens listing the train tracks, I crane my neck to read it before looking back down at the person standing next to me. It's Sarah.

"Hey!" I say, turning to her. "Where are you headed?"

"The city. There's a flea market in Williamsburg that has the best deals for vintage clothing and handmade goods from artists. You'd really like it," she says, then pauses. "Plus, there's a really good food market there. Ever had a ramen burger?"

"A *ramen burger*?" I repeat.

"Don't look so skeptical, they're a-mazing."

I laugh. "I mean, I like both of those things separately, so . . . maybe I'll be into it? I'll have to try that sometime."

"Trust me. You won't regret it. What about you? What're you going into the city for?" she asks, as she eyes Andy buying his ticket. I don't want to get into the paper hearts so I tell her the same white lie I told my mom.

"I got into a school in New York so I'm going to check it out."

"Oh no way, what school? I'm going to Columbia next year."

"You are?" I ask. "I might be too. I was thinking about deferring for a year, though. . . ." I trail off. If I'm being honest with myself, I thought about college way too much when it didn't matter and ironically now that it does, I haven't at all. That's the thing—sometimes it's hard to think about the future when you're stuck in the past.

"Well, if you don't defer, we could start school together,"

Sarah says hopefully, but she must see a look on my face because she adds on, "Just ignore me. I'm just so excited to get out of this town. I want college to start as soon as possible."

"I get that," I say. "I'll let you know what I do. . . . It would . . . it would actually be really nice to know someone."

Sarah smiles as Andy comes up behind me. "Well, I'll let you enjoy your college tour, then." Thankfully, Andy doesn't correct her.

"Do you want to sit with us?" I ask.

For a second, she looks happy, but then she shakes her head. "I'm sitting in the Quiet Car. Either reading the sixth Harry Potter book for the twentieth time or starting a new Game of Thrones."

"Both better options than sitting with us," Andy says. "I plan on distracting Ella the entire way."

I turn to Sarah. "Maybe I *should* be sitting with you."

The two of them laugh, but part of me was completely serious. If it weren't for the paper hearts, I would love to be heading to the city with Sarah to shop and eat a ramen burger. That sounds way better than what I'd normally be doing by myself. I like that she's not afraid to do things alone. Whenever I want to do something, I feel like I need to go with a group of friends or at least one other person, which is a shame, because there are things that sometimes I don't get to do because people are busy. Sarah just seems so independent and sure of herself.

Here she is, doing a day trip to Brooklyn on her own like it's no big deal.

I wish I could be more like that, I think as Andy and I board the train.

~

Traveling to NYC sometimes feels like I'm journeying to some faraway land. Today it feels even more so. The tracks run parallel to the Hudson River, which is now partially frozen and covered in snow from last night. It would be extremely peaceful if Andy would stop talking.

Maybe I really should've sat in the Quiet Car.

"Do you think someone will try to sit with us?" he asks now, nodding toward the seat to his right. We're in a three-seater.

"Maybe. The train gets crowded on weekends."

He shakes his head. "I should've brought iced coffee."

"It's February. Why an *iced* coffee?

"First of all, I'm not a wimp, Ella. I can drink iced coffee any time of the year. People don't start drinking warm water because we're in the dead of winter. Second of all, the iced coffee is a ploy so nobody would want to sit with us. I have this trick that I'm debating telling you about on account of how you'll finally know I'm an evil genius."

I roll my eyes. "Do I even want to know, after your Hot Chocolate Theory?"

"Hmm. Well, you seem smart but not very evil. I don't want to be a bad influence on you."

I shake my head. "Just tell me."

"Okay, so if I had an iced coffee, I could hold it right here," he says, holding the pretend coffee in the imaginary line between this seat and the one over. "And I'd let the condensation from my iced coffee drip ever so slowly onto the next seat. Then as people walk by, they will think *Oh, there's an open seat!* But they will come by to see there's in fact water on that seat tainted by my drink and keep moving because who on earth wants to have a wet butt from some nerd's iced coffee? I'll tell you," he says, pausing for dramatic effect. "No one."

I stare at him in disbelief. "That *is* an evil genius move," I finally say.

He grins, his dimple showing. "Now your turn."

"Turn for what? I never said I was an evil genius."

"Okay, well, you don't have to tell me what makes you diabolical, but tell me what makes you a little less perfect than the good-girl image you're still giving off to me now."

"I do *not* have a good-girl image," I argue.

He raises an eyebrow. "I can see for this trip you came prepared with celery sticks . . . and is that a PB&J cut into a heart?" he asks, peering inside my purse.

I zip it shut. "Don't even think of asking for snacks later if you get hungry."

"I won't," he says. "I'll just ask you about your five-year plan."

I look out the window.

"Oh my God, you *do* have a five-year plan. Now you have to tell me. I'm intrigued. Do you think about it while you cut your snacks into hearts?" he asks in a teasing voice.

"It's perfectly normal to have a five-year plan," I argue.

"I never said it wasn't. But a lot of people our age don't have one."

"You don't strike me as someone who does what everyone does," I say.

"Touché," he says. "Okay, but seriously. Can you tell me now? I'm really curious."

I pause, examining his eyes. They are no longer teasing— he seems sincere.

"Well, in five years I hope to be graduating from college, or at least that's the plan now," I start to say. "And don't laugh . . . but my dream is to combine my love of books with my love of planning and become a book publicist."

"Why would I laugh at that?" he asks. "That sounds like an awesome dream."

"Really?"

"Yeah, I can totally see you doing that. What made you think of being a publicist?"

"In the back of books, authors always thank their publicists in the acknowledgments. That's where I first got the idea. Plus, I always thought it would be fun to plan big book launches in New York City for my favorite writers."

Andy smiles at me in a way I haven't seen him smile at me yet. "That's great. You're lucky to know what you're passionate about already. I have no idea what I want to do. I never even know what I want to do when I get out of bed in the morning, let alone in five years."

"Well, did you want to be anything when you grew up?"

"Yeah, when I was a kid I was convinced I'd be drafted into the NHL. I always loved hockey. It was heartbreaking, though. I tore my ACL and had to stop skating for a while."

"Wait a second, that's not true," I say, crossing my arms. "When we went ice-skating you were shaking like a leaf."

His cheeks turn red. "Okay, I *was* nervous but not why you think. That was the first time I've put skates back on since the accident."

My jaw drops. "Really? Why didn't you say something? You didn't have to—"

"That's exactly why I didn't want to tell you. I wanted to skate with you. I'm glad I did it even though I was scared the whole time just remembering how it happened. . . ."

Suddenly, my mind flashes back to how slow he was at the beginning. How he was petrified of running into that little girl and hurting her . . .

"I wasn't like a star or anything," he says. "To be clear, since you normally associate with Pete Yearling. But I was interested in playing in college somewhere. Probably D3. But after my injury all the interested coaches dropped me."

"That's awful," I say.

"Tell me about it. My whole life was leading up to one thing, and then in one second, everything changed for me."

"Wow," I say.

What he is saying reminds me of myself in a lot of ways— I'm still afraid to get back behind the wheel. Maybe we have more in common than I thought.

"Yeah, but don't feel sorry for me. I had surgery, and I'm pretty much all healed now."

"So how come you don't play hockey again?"

He shrugs. "I've thought about it. I might try to walk onto a team next year, wherever I end up going, on my own. Until then, I'm just trying to take care of myself. But it's weird . . . I've spent my whole life doing this one thing, and now I have the chance to do so much other stuff."

"Like what?" I pry.

"Well, work, for one. I can read more, for another, and not just for school. And going on spur-of the-moment adventures is definitely a plus. Aren't you glad I don't have practice today?"

I laugh. "Touché." But in that moment, I really am glad he's here.

"In all seriousness," he starts, looking out the window, "I kind of like that life is like a train ride. You have to make some stops along the way to your destination."

"Did you just come up with that?" I laugh.

"I did." He smiles, and his dimple comes out. "Did it sound good?"

"Definitely less cheesy than saying you're the conductor of your own journey."

"Oh come on. I hope you like cheese. You can call me Gouda."

I roll my eyes at him but he laughs. "So, what about you? Have there been any stops on your journey?"

I nod.

"You're not going to tell me that, though, are you?" he asks.

"Nope."

But later when I get hungry for my snacks, I offer Andy a celery stick.

~

After we arrive in NYC, we stream out of the train into Grand Central Terminal and find our way to the subway.

It's only when we get outside that I let out a large breath in the cold air. A little puff that looks like a miniature cloud escapes my lips.

We head to Central Park, which is exactly where it sounds like it'll be: in the center of the city. On the way there Andy tells me that the rocks and boulders in the park are left over from the Ice Age, and when Manhattan was being built, everything was constructed around them. His eyes light up as he tells me, like they always do when he shares one of his fun facts. I decide that might be my favorite thing about him as we walk together now.

NYC really is magical this time of year. The streets seem quieter. Maybe because of the snow. The sidewalk has been cleared, but mounds of snow line the streets and white powder dusts the trees and traffic signs.

The paths in the park have also been shoveled. Once we enter, we follow one toward the castle at the top of a hill. Below it, there's a small pond, completely frozen. On the way up the hill, I tell Andy that Belvedere means *beautiful view* in Italian. He raises his eyebrows at me as if to say he's impressed. I'm glad I finally get to tell him a fun fact he didn't know.

As I near the castle, I am blown away by the view. It makes me think that this is a place I would've wanted to go to with someone special. Suddenly, I'm kicking myself for not asking Pete more questions—I should've asked him about the Polaroid.

I pull out my phone to text him and see that he already sent a text this morning.

I had a great time last night.

I respond.

Me too! ☺

After I press send, I start typing my next text.

> Random question . . . did we ever go to
> Belvedere Castle together?

I stare at the text for a couple seconds. Knowing this simple answer could finally give the closure I need, but it would ruin everything with the paper hearts. Why can't I just be patient? I only have five to go. I'm sure I'll find out the reason for everything at the end of this.

I delete the text and put my phone back in my pocket.

When I look up, Andy's shaking his head at me.

"Was wondering when you were going to put that away. We're practically there, you know," he says, with his cocky smirk.

"I *know*," I say.

The stone castle towers in front of us. Its intricate arches are covered in snow and look like they're from another century. Streetlamps in front must light up the castle at night for everyone to see. I let out a deep sigh, thinking about the Polaroid picture.

"What're you thinking?" Andy asks.

"Oh, nothing," I say, but then think of something. "What's the number on the paper heart, again?"

"Six."

I nod, looking from Andy back to the castle. What on earth could six have to do with anything? I look up to start counting the windows and see people on top of the castle, peering over the stone wall.

"Do we go up?" I ask.

Andy nods. "Maybe we have to look to six o'clock or something?"

"That's not a bad idea."

"Wow," Andy says.

"What?" I ask, starting for the entrance.

"Nothing. I just like to bask in my compliments from you."

I laugh. "I said it's not a bad idea. I take back the compliment if you're wrong."

"That's not how compliments work."

"Sure it is," I argue.

We make our way through the entrance and then up the steep winding staircase. At the top, we are let out onto a terrace with a clear view of Central Park and the Manhattan skyline.

"Which way is six o'clock?" I ask, making my way to the edge.

Beyond the icy pond are snow-covered trees, and people the size of my thumb roaming the park. I'm about to say we need to think of something else when Andy comes up next to me.

"Whoa, this is incredible," he says. "When you said *Belvedere* means 'beautiful view,' I assumed it was referring to the castle itself. But this view is incredible."

I look out again at the six o'clock angle. I run my hand along the rail, searching for a paper heart. I even bend down to see if there are any hidden cracks where my admirer could've stuffed the next heart.

My shoulders slump as I stand back up. I really hoped Andy was right, but he doesn't seem to care.

"That's the Delacorte Theater," he says, pointing to a snow-covered amphitheater. "In the summer there are free Shakespeare performances there. And that over there looks like a baseball field," he says, now moving his hand to an area off in the distance surrounded by gates.

"Remember how I said I could take your compliment away?" I ask.

He frowns. "We're already up here. We might as well take it all in."

"I know you're going to tell me that Sherlock Holmes doesn't look for clues, he just looks," I say, sighing. "But please don't. All I want is to find this paper heart."

It's pathetic, I know. Here I am in this beautiful castle in the middle of New York City with one of the most incredible views I've ever seen and I'm focused on finding a flimsy piece of paper.

Andy looks to me. "We'll find it," he assures me. "Just relax for a second."

The funny thing about having someone tell you to relax

is that it always has the opposite effect. I want to say *I am relaxed,* but arguing will make me look tense. Suddenly, I feel all wound up, like the castle's winding staircase. Andy's eyes are calm, though, as he looks off the balcony.

"Whenever I see people from far away, or from up above like we are now, the small people remind me of illustrations in a children's book," Andy starts to say. "I like to give them stories."

For a second, I think he's kidding in his typical Andy way, but he's looking out onto the stretch of emptiness in front of us.

"There are little people everywhere going about their lives, like we are," Andy continues. "Like that family over there—do you see them?"

I follow his pointing finger to a family of four playing in the snow. One little kid is running around and another is building something. Maybe a snowman, but it's hard to tell from so far away.

"What's their story?" he asks me.

"Uh . . . they're a family playing in the snow?"

"Oh, come on. I know you have more of an imagination than that."

I roll my eyes at him.

"Don't roll your eyes at me. You're not even trying!"

"Fine," I say, looking back at the family. "The mom has lost something important. A necklace, maybe . . . or actually, her wedding ring."

"Which one?" Andy asks. "They create very different stories."

"Wedding ring," I decide. "That's why the boy is digging in the snow. He's searching for it. The other boy is running around because he's panicking." I stop my story, looking to him for approval. He steps closer to me to see what I'm looking at before turning to me.

"Why are Mom and Dad still next to each other?" he asks.

"The dad is comforting her," I suggest.

"Why would he comfort her if it's her fault?" Andy asks.

"Because this is a make-believe story and I say so," I answer.

Andy laughs. "Well, in your fictional story, why is he comforting her?"

I look at the couple again. His arm is around her shoulder.

"He wants her to know it's okay. She didn't mean to lose the ring. He still loves her, and that's more important than what she lost. The ring isn't as important as the memories," I finish.

"Why?" Andy asks again.

"Because memories are the most important thing there is," I say with a shakier voice than I intend to. I'm not sad, exactly; I think more than anything I'm surprised that I'm finally able to put into words why my memory loss has been affecting me as much as it has.

He looks at me and then focuses on my lips, and for a second I could swear he wants to kiss me. But then his eyes dart back to mine.

"What?" I ask, because he has been staring at me for a second too long.

He grins at me. "I think they're just a family playing in the snow," he finally says.

"You're impossible." I laugh. "Why did you want me to make up that whole story?"

"It's fun to watch you squirm. Plus, it was a good story. I'd recommend it at the library."

I punch him in the arm. "Quit distracting me and help me find this paper heart!"

He grabs his arm where I hit him like it hurt even though it wasn't even that hard. "My idea was a bad one. Why don't *you* come up with something now?"

"I'm trying!" I huff, growing frustrated. "It just doesn't make sense. Nothing is labeled six."

"Well, maybe this clue is supposed to be different," Andy says.

"Maybe you're a know-it-all," I say.

"Why, thanks for admitting *I know it all*," he teases, but I'm already walking away.

"Where are you going?" he asks.

I shrug. "I'm going to go all the way back out to the entrance and retrace our steps. Maybe we missed something. Why don't you keep looking up here?"

"You want to split up?" he asks. He sounds hurt.

"Just really quickly," I say. "I'll meet you back up here."

I turn and walk down the winding staircase toward the front, where the lampposts stand. Before I left home this morning, I stashed the Polaroid in my coat pocket. I pull it out now and look at it. In the picture, I'm leaning on a lamppost in front of a stone ledge, with trees in the background. Scanning the different lampposts around me, I find one that looks like it could be the one in the picture.

I make my way over. For some reason I have the urge to reach out and touch the lamppost, like I'm doing in the Polaroid. Maybe in the back of my mind I hope that touching it will zap my memory back like a lightning bolt. Maybe that's the real reason I wanted to leave Andy.

But nothing happens when I finally touch the pole. All I can feel is the cold metal underneath my gloves.

I have the urge to kick the snow against the stone wall. I came all this way for nothing. I feel a sob about to escape, so I quickly start moving again toward the side tower. Then I look around the sixth wooden arch. Nothing.

What if there was supposed to be a paper heart here, though? What if my admirer put it here and someone found it before me or it blew away in the snow? Or maybe I'm just flat-out wrong again. Maybe this is all just a waste of time. What if I never get my memories back?

I shake my head. I can't think about those possibilities yet. I make my way back to the castle's entrance. There's a couple in front of me walking slowly and holding hands, so there's no way to pass them. I can tell from their first few steps that they're in no hurry. By the time the stairwell starts to wind, I try to block out how many steps we have left to go.

And that's when I have an idea.

I rush back to the bottom of the steps and begin to walk back up the stairs, counting as I go. *One, two, three . . .*

When I make it to the sixth step, I crouch down and feel underneath the metal stair. Then finally I feel it—paper.

I tug gently, and suddenly there's a paper heart in my hand.

"Check Yes Juliet" ♥ *We the Kings*

"Unwritten" ♥ *Natasha Bedingfield*

"Head over Feet" ♥ *Alanis Morissette*

"Listen to Your Heart" ♥ *Roxette*

"Higher Love" ♥ *Whitney Houston*

"A Thousand Years" ♥ *Christina Perri*

"P.S. I Love You" ♥ *The Beatles*

"The Letter" ♥ *Joe Cocker*

"Paper Rings" ♥ *Taylor Swift*

"Strawberry Letter Number 23" ♥ *The Brothers Johnson*

"Kiss Me" ♥ Sixpence None the Richer

"Valentine Girl" ♥ New Kids on the Block

"Signed, Sealed, Delivered" ♥ Stevie Wonder

"Classic" ♥ The Knocks

"A Thousand Miles" ♥ Vanessa Carlton

"Will You Still Love Me Tomorrow?" ♥ Carole King

"Paper Hearts" ♥ The Vamps

"Falling for You" ♥ Colbie Caillat

"Wonderwall" ♥ Oasis

"Love Letters" ♥ Aretha Franklin

"I'm Yours" ♥ Jason Mraz

"A World Alone" ♥ Lorde

"Love Song" ♥ Sara Bareilles

"God Must Have Spent a Little More Time on You"
♥ *NSYNC

"Then" ♥ Brad Paisley

"Yellow Lights" ♥ Harry Hudson

"Love Me Like You Do" ♥ Ellie Goulding

"Red Roses" ♥ Laundry Day

"Love Letters" ♥ Elvis Presley

"Photograph" ♥ Ed Sheeran

"My Paper Heart" ♥ The All-American Rejects

"Ocean Eyes" ♥ Billie Eilish

Chapter 15

"WE'RE HERE ANYWAY. I JUST WANT TO SEE THIS ONE THING before we leave," Andy says for the third time on the subway back to Grand Central to catch our train.

"I need to go home to listen to these songs," I say, also for the third time.

Suddenly, Andy pulls AirPods out of his pocket. I raise an eyebrow at him.

"You've had those with you this whole time?"

He nods. "And I'll download those songs for you too, so you can listen on the train ride back . . . under one condition."

"What?" I ask impatiently.

"You'll go to the Whispering Gallery with me. I've always wanted to check it out."

I shake my head. "One, I have no idea what that is. And

two, we're practically at Grand Central. We'll miss the train if we go anywhere."

He grins. "The Whispering Gallery is *inside* Grand Central," he says, shaking the AirPods in my face. "Do we have a deal?"

I pause. I really want to listen to these songs. I grab the earbuds out of his hand before responding. "Deal."

"Good. Maybe I'll forgive you for finding that last clue without me."

"I said I was sorry," I say. "I just needed to think on my own for a second."

He nods. "Got it. For the record, I'm only teasing. Besides, I witnessed a proposal, which was pretty cool. Turns out it was a good thing I was alone."

"A marriage proposal?" I ask.

"Yeah," he says, whipping out his phone. "I took a couple pics that I sent to them afterward. They were so grateful someone was there to capture the moment."

I look down at the phone in his hands. There's a guy on his knees and a young woman with her hands covering her mouth in pure shock. But it's not the proposal that's shocking to me—it's that I recognize them. I'm staring at the couple I almost bulldozed on the winding staircase. Suddenly, I'm relieved I didn't do anything to put a damper on their seemingly perfect day. I guess you really never know when a moment is going to be significant.

For some reason, it makes me think of the moments leading up to my accident. I wonder if I would have done anything differently if I had known the accident was coming. I immediately think yes. I definitely would've fixed whatever was going on with Carmen. I wouldn't have rudely texted during my nail appointment with Sydney. I would have told Ashley and my parents I love them. Sometimes I think about asking each of them what the last thing I said to them was, but part of me doesn't want to know in case it was bad.

Still, for all the bad moments in life, I know there are so many good ones I can have. I look down at the photo of the woman getting proposed to and I can't help but smile. I wonder about all the moments they had leading up to this one: the moment they met, their first date, the first time they said I love you to each other. All the moments I'm looking forward to for myself.

"I saw that couple walking in," I say to Andy. "That's amazing."

"There's a few more," he says. He scrolls through his phone. He shows me a few photos of the young man and woman posed in front of the rail. As he continues to scroll, I see a picture of me for a split second before he scrolls back in the opposite direction.

"Wait a second, what was that?" I ask.

His cheeks turn red. "It was nothing. I took a picture of you when you were gazing over the rail. It almost looks like you're a model."

I'm definitely not a model, but even I can see what he means.

He took the photo when I wasn't looking. The backdrop—the Manhattan skyline combined with the perfect snow on the ground—makes my pose and my pensive expression look staged. But I didn't even know he was taking the picture. I wonder why he did.

Suddenly, the subway stops. "This is us," Andy says. "Now off to the Whispering Gallery so you can whisper sweet nothings to me for taking that photo."

Andy leads me to the lower level of the terminal.

"Are we getting oysters?" I ask, seeing the Oyster Bar restaurant next to us.

Andy smiles at me. "No. *This* is the Whispering Gallery."

I look around. There's nothing around us, aside from the intricately tiled walls and ceiling.

Andy keeps walking, though, so I follow him. He stops in front of an arch.

"Stay here," he instructs me. "I'm going to go diagonally from you."

"What . . . ," I start, but he's already walking away. I stand awkwardly as people pass me by.

But if I'm at all self-conscious about people looking at me, it stops immediately. This is nothing like high school. People here are too focused on getting to their destinations to stop and stare at me, even if I'm standing alone in a corner.

"Ella, can you hear me?"

The voice comes from the walls, but I know it's Andy's. I

spin around and see that he's standing at a matching arch on the other end of the passageway. He waves at me and then turns back to the wall.

"I'll take that as a yes," he says. My jaw drops. I can hear him like he's inches away. Talking to him now across a space like this reminds me of when Ashley and I were younger, before the days of cell phones, and we'd communicate from our separate rooms with walkie-talkies. At the time, it felt like magic. This feels pretty close to it.

"How is this possible?" I ask in amazement. I realize it looks like I'm talking to a wall, but I don't care. For a moment I wonder if he'll be able to hear me, but then he responds.

"The architecture. The curved walls bend the reflection of your voice. It's an acoustic phenomenon."

"How did you learn about this place? I've been to Grand Central a bunch of times and I never knew this existed."

"I read about it. I'm glad you like it, but can I hear my sweet nothings now?"

I give him an eye roll, but I realize of course he's not going to see it. "I'm not sure you deserve sweet nothings. It's not that great a photo," I say.

"I think the Whispering Gallery is broken," Andy says.

"Why, you can't hear me?" I ask before spinning around to see him.

"I thought I heard you say 'it's not that great a photo.' But you look beautiful."

At that moment, I'm glad Andy is so far away from me that he can't see me blush. There's a long pause before I hear him speak again.

"Are you always this bad with compliments?" he asks.

"Maybe," I say.

"Okay, we can save all the compliments for me, then," he says, making me laugh. "But if you're not going to whisper sweet nothings to me, how about you share one secret?"

I pause. "What kind of secret?"

"I don't know. Something you want to whisper into these walls that we'll never talk about."

I can tell by his tone that he's grinning. His dimple is showing. It's amazing that I can know this from across such a vast space.

What does Andy not know about me that I can share now?

Obviously, the big thing comes to mind. The reason we're here.

I stare at the arch in front of me. It looks like nothing special—just a wall. But I realize that's what the paper hearts must seem like to Andy: Nothing important. Pieces of paper directing me to new places. What he doesn't realize is that the hearts mean so much more than they say.

Maybe that's a secret worth sharing.

"Okay," I begin. "I haven't told you this yet. . . ." I trail off.

"That *is* what a secret is," Andy says when I don't finish.

I smile. "I know. It's hard for me to say."

"Sorry, I won't interrupt you again. I promise."

He sounds sincere. The sincerest I've ever heard him. After a long pause, the words roll out.

"I was in a car accident about a year ago," I say easily. Maybe it's because I'm talking to a wall, not to Andy directly. Thinking about him hearing me makes my heart speed up. "And I have retrograde amnesia. I can't remember eleven weeks of my life, and I don't know if I'll ever get them back. I know in the grand scheme of things I'm lucky and it's not a big deal . . ." I trail off again.

"It *is* a big deal," I hear Andy say. "Sorry, I promised I wasn't going to interrupt you."

"Don't worry," I say. "It's also okay that you've been making fun of these paper hearts. If I were you, I probably would too. But I guess my secret is the real reason I'm following these paper hearts—I hope I can get my memory back. That's what the first one alluded to, anyway."

As soon as I say it out loud, a weight lifts from my chest. Almost as if I just went to Confession. I let out a large breath that I hope Andy can't hear.

"Okay, that was my secret. You can say something now," I say. I expect him to start rambling right away, but there's nothing. For a moment, I think maybe the wall has actually stopped working this time. What if Andy didn't even hear me? But then I feel a tap on my shoulder.

I turn, and standing right behind me is Andy. "I thought

you couldn't hear me for a sec—" I say, spinning around, but before I can finish, his arms are around me. He's hugging me right in the middle of Grand Central Terminal. I don't care about people watching or about anything else around us. All I can sense are his hands gripping my back. He's squeezing tightly, like he's trying to press out any worry I have, and all I can do is hug him too. When I do, my face presses into his chest and I can smell his cologne through his parka. It's soothing, just like his sturdy palms on my back.

Eventually he breaks the silence. "Don't be so concerned with your past and your future that you forget how utterly incredible you are right now," he whispers.

When he releases me, I feel a little dazed but mostly grateful.

It's a hug I didn't know I needed.

On the train, I hand Andy my paper heart and watch him download the songs to his phone. He puts them in an album he creates, called *Paper Hearts Playlist.*

Once he's done, he gives me one of his AirPods and puts the other in his own ear. We sit listening to the love songs. Some are upbeat and lively; others are slower, with a hint of heartbreak. Andy has a corny way of bopping to the music that makes me laugh. He knows way more of the songs than I do.

"Can I ask a question?" I say, and Andy nods, removing his AirPod. "How do you know all these?" I ask.

"My dad was a big music guy," he answers. "I mean, is. But now that we don't live together, I don't hear him blasting music in the shower anymore. I used to get so annoyed because it would wake me up in the morning, but now I kind of miss it."

I nod. There are plenty of annoying things about my family that I'd probably miss if they were suddenly gone.

"You should tell him you miss that. I bet he'd appreciate it."

He studies my face before saying, "Yeah, I should."

Then he takes the AirPod out of my ear. "I know I said I wouldn't talk about it . . . but what you said at the Whispering Gallery . . . Well, I really appreciate you telling me what you did back there."

He smiles and puts the AirPod back in my ear, brushing my cheek as he does. My chest tightens. With the buds back in our ears, the music starts playing again.

When we're about halfway through our journey, we start the playlist over again. It's an unspoken agreement.

Soon I feel my eyes grow heavy. Before I know it, I feel Andy tapping my shoulder. I open my eyes to see him staring down at me. My face is completely plastered to his shoulder. I must have passed out and used him as a pillow. Thank God there's no drool on his shirt. Or maybe there *is*, since he's smiling at me like he's about to tease me.

"We're home," Andy says.

I jump up in my seat. "Sorry."

"Don't worry about it. I'm impressed by your ability to sleep like that."

I am too. Looking at him now, all the memories of the day come flashing back to me, including telling him about my accident, and the way he brought my body to his when he hugged me.

"Let's go," I say without looking at him.

"Wait," Andy says.

I think he's going to tell me not to be like this, that it's okay to let my guard down, but he doesn't. He looks at me softly until finally he smiles.

"You still have my AirPod."

I shake my head. "Oh, right." I pull it out of my ear and hand it to him.

Our hands touch for only a brief second, but I suddenly have this weird feeling. A desire, really. Because when Andy looks at me again, it's as if I'm still snow in December.

Chapter 16

I'VE HAD PLENTY OF CRUSHES. THE KIND THAT HIT YOU THE second you meet them. They're called crushes for a reason. All of a sudden it feels like your heart is being squeezed, and it's either because you're about to explode with happiness or because you're about to break into a thousand pieces.

Obviously, I crush hard.

But as Andy drives me home from the train station, I know this isn't like my crush on Adam in elementary school, which started immediately after he shared his paints with me in art class. This is different.

Maybe a crush can be like a book you find at the library. First you're drawn in by the cover. Then you try to find out what it's about, so you read the little description on the jacket. Maybe it says exactly what you want to read, or maybe it's mysteriously vague and it makes you even more curious. Either way, you decide that you're going to choose this book knowing very little about it, but you have this excited feeling that if you dive in, you might be swept away. That's the feeling I'm suddenly getting with Andy.

He's like a story I can't wait to read.

But what about my admirer?

I feel a surge of guilt just thinking about the paper hearts as soon as Andy pulls up in my driveway. The car stops and he undoes his seat belt.

"Where are you going?" I ask. He beats me at unbuckling our seat belts.

"Walking you to your door."

This wasn't a date—not a real one—so I didn't even anticipate that he'd want to walk me. Maybe he's not so jaded after all.

"Is that . . . okay?" he asks. My face must say it's not. But really that's because I've just decided that I might have a crush and now he's volunteering to walk me to my door and I'm trying not to smile too hard. Could this mean he likes me too? What he said at the Whispering Gallery made it seem like he did, but he could just have been trying to be nice after I told him my big secret.

"Of course it's okay," I say.

We get out of the car and walk together toward my front door. I'm careful to not trip over my own feet, which happens sometimes when I'm nervous. It's even more of a possibility now, because it looks like somebody tried to shovel the walk-way after last night's snow, but there's still a slick layer of ice they weren't able to chip at.

"Be careful," I joke to him. "We know what happened the last time you went ice-skating."

He grins. "Are you going to beat me again?"

"Duh," I say, smiling back. But I don't actually speed up. I want this short walk to the door to last.

When we reach the door, I pull the keys out of my bag. They jingle awkwardly in my hand. I'm stalling, but I don't know why. Maybe I'm waiting for Andy to hint that he's feeling the same way.

I look at him and he's staring at me, smiling.

"What?"

"I'm just relishing this moment. It's the first time you're paying more attention to me than to a paper heart."

"Paper hear—" I start to say, whipping my head around to the door, then stopping short: because right there in front of my eyes is another letter taped to the door.

"Never mind," Andy says. I turn back to him and watch his shoulders sink.

There's a moment when neither of us know what to say. Eventually, he clears his throat. "Well, now that you see the heart, are you going to read it?" He sounds irritated.

"Oh, yeah," I say, not bothering to try to make him less ir-ritated. I'm annoyed too—at myself. Here I am, off gallivanting with Andy, when there could be a guy out there sending me on a romantic scavenger hunt. I suddenly feel like a horrible, stupid person.

I snatch the paper heart off the door and unfold it. Inside, there are two tickets for a chocolate-making class at the Culinary Institute of America, where some of the best chefs and bakers in the country are trained. I didn't know they had classes for people like me. There's a restaurant there that I've been to on special occasions, like when I got into Columbia. Everything about the CIA feels fancy, including the message with the tickets.

Whether you dream of truffles, a dense and rich flourless chocolate cake, or light-as-air-soufflés, this chocolate lover's class will teach you the essential techniques needed to make irresistible desserts. Learn tricks of the trade from a CIA chef while making a sweet surprise!

Suddenly, my stomach lurches. There had been plenty of sweet shop vendors at the Hudson Valley Orchard. I can't remember exactly, but I'm pretty sure I told Pete I wished I had saved room for dessert but I was too chocolated out from the hot chocolate. Did he remember me saying that?

"What a coincidence," Andy says, interrupting my thoughts. "Chocolate is my favorite food group."

I shake my head. There's no way he can come with me to this next clue. It was harmless when he was just some by-stander giving me rides, but now . . . it's bad enough as it is. I expect Andy to argue or have some comeback, but he nods.

"I figured."

Well, that was easy, at least.

"Thanks for today," I say, because I mean it, and none of this is his fault. Sometimes it just feels like I'm ungrateful. I remember what Carmen said about me being a bad friend around the time of the accident. Why don't I ever learn?

"Wait, El, are you ok—" Andy starts, but I turn before he can see a tear roll down my cheek.

"See you around," I say, quickly opening the door and shutting it behind me firmly, like a book I no longer want to finish. Or at least have to stop reading for now.

~

Once I get inside, I check my phone and see a couple of missed FaceTimes and a text from Carmen.

Um excuse me. Are you going to tell me how the date went? I'm dying over here!

For a second, I wonder how she could possibly know I was on a date with Andy. And then I shake my head. She's talking about my date with Pete, of course. How quickly I forgot.

I want to FaceTime her back, but she'll know from the look on my face that something is up. Part of me thinks I should just tell her everything about the paper hearts, but another part knows I don't have the energy to right now. Instead, I text back.

> It was a lot of fun. He was sweet. Kiss at the end was
> even sweeter.

She texts back immediately.

OH MY GOD. TELL ME MORE.

Do you think he'll take you on another date?

This is the first time we've both had boys. WE CAN
DOUBLE.

Despite how low I felt moments ago, her excitement makes me crack a small smile. Then it gives me an idea to make things right again.

I text Pete.

> Hey! I'm going to this chocolate class tomorrow and have
> an extra ticket if you're interested.

I keep it vague in case he's not actually my admirer.
He responds immediately.

A class about CHOCOLATE? Of course I'm interested.

It's a nice text, which makes me feel even worse for how I've been acting. I have to make it up to him.

Great. Pick me up at noon?

Can't wait.

Same, I text back, even though I can't help but feel that I'm not being entirely honest. When I was with Andy, I had this feeling of wanting to know more about him. With Pete, I had a feeling of familiarity, which isn't exactly bad—there are plenty of things I love that are familiar. The familiar smell of burning wood when my dad starts a fire in the winter. The familiar joy I have when my favorite song starts playing on Spotify.

Familiar can be good, I remind myself.

Chapter 17

THE NEXT MORNING I'M WOKEN UP BY A KNOCK ON MY door. Before I say anything, Ashley barges in. She's wearing leggings and a zip-up jacket.

"Do you know where my running gloves are?" she asks.

"No. Why would I?"

She shrugs. "Maybe because I found my jacket in your room yesterday."

Whoops. Busted.

"Well, if I find my gloves, do you want to come with me?" she asks.

"For a run?"

"No, to prom." She smiles sarcastically.

"Sure," I say, surprised she wants to run with me. I haven't gone on a run with her since before my accident, and I know I'm not exactly in shape from the hike at Breakneck.

"I might slow you dow—" I start.

"Be ready in five minutes," she says before leaving me lying in my bed. Eventually, I roll out from under my covers to investigate my closet. My running clothes are way in the back, because they haven't been used since last year.

Some people don't like running in the cold, but I'd much rather bundle up and run outside in the winter than sweat a gallon in the heat of summer. I find warm running tights and a fleece jacket.

My run with Ashley isn't the longest one I've ever been on, but it's nice to clear my head.

"What're you up to today?" Ashley asks once we're back in the driveway. I'm gasping for air, my hands on my hips as we slow to a stop.

Between deep breaths, I realize I haven't filled her in about anything with Andy. It's probably for the best. If I told her I was hanging out with him yesterday, she'd have a million questions about him. Now I can just tell her about Pete.

"I'm going to the Culinary today for a chocolate-making class," I say. "With Pete."

"Oh," Ashley said softly, as if she's bummed. Did she think we were going to keep hanging out?

"Sorry," I say right away. "Where's Steve? Don't you normally hang out with him on weekends?"

"Why do you always bring Steve into everything?"

I gawk. "I guess that's a no. . . ." I think back to when I

mentioned him earlier. She brushed it off then too. "Did something happen?" I ask.

"No, nothing happened. Is it that unbelievable that I'd want to hang out with my sister?"

I look at her in amazement. The truth is yes, it *is* unbelievable. Maybe last year I would've thought otherwise, but I can't think of a single time recently that she chose me over Steve.

"Why aren't you saying anything?" Ashley demands.

"I'm thinking about how to respond without being mean," I admit.

Her head whips back like I said something horrible.

"You're one to talk, Ella. You're going to a chocolate-making class with an *ex-boyfriend* over me."

"That's not fair. He's not just my ex-boyfriend," I argue, before I realize that wasn't the point. "I would've invited you if I knew you wanted to come."

"Yeah, right" is all she says, and she storms away toward the stairs.

"How are *you* mad at *me*?" I call out. "You always do stuff with Steve over me!"

It was about time I told her the truth, but I never thought it would be in a fight like this. She doesn't even turn around to talk about it. She continues storming toward the steps, even past our dad as he walks out of the office without a word.

"What's her deal?" I ask Dad as we listen to her feet go up

the stairs. There must be something going on with Steve that she's not telling me.

My dad shrugs. "I was hoping you could fill me in."

I sigh. Somehow, I'm still messing everything up.

~

When I open the door, I notice Pete's haircut immediately. His sandy brown hair is short. I always liked the flow to his long locks, but there's something about this that works for him. He's clean-cut.

Pete strokes the top of his head as he catches me staring. "The barber went a little overboard. . . ."

"No, I love it," I respond.

"You do?" he asks. It isn't the question that bothers me, it's how he says it. Like it's hard to believe I wouldn't like something about him, even if it's just a simple haircut. If Pete is my admirer, the least I could do is show some appreciation. Even if he isn't, this great guy is clearly into me. Friday night, he joined me for a cheesy date that a lot of guys would probably laugh at. He could've come up with a million and one excuses for why we couldn't do it, or offered to hang out later, but he didn't. It could be because the chocolate date was his idea to begin with, or because he just wants to hang out with me. Either way, it makes him a great guy. He's at my doorstep looking down at me, surprised that I'm complimenting him.

"Really," I say. "You look great. And thanks so much for coming with me today. It means a lot."

"Of course," he says, his smile widening. "I'm happy you asked me."

"Still *sweet* of you to join me," I say, starting to walk toward his car.

He nods, missing my pun entirely, but I won't let that bother me today.

~

Walking into the Culinary Institute of America is a little like walking into your favorite reality cooking show. You can smell the classrooms before you even enter the building, since half of them are actually test kitchens. We'll be meeting in one of them, and as I make my way toward it with Pete, I get a delicious whiff of something cinnamon. My brain tries to guess what it is while my mouth waters. Maybe apple pie or some other delicious pastry? Peering into the test kitchen windows, I can see the shiny copper pots hanging from the ceilings like decorations. In my pure excitement, I grab Pete's arm as we walk, and he smiles sweetly back at me.

Just when I think I'm about to have the best sequel to a first date ever, I walk into the test kitchen, and there, standing by a table in the back, is Andy.

My cheeks burn. *You've got to be kidding me.*

I let go of Pete's arm and walk straight over to him. It's only when I'm right in front of him that I realize he's not the only person I recognize. Sarah's sitting next to him, wearing a striped turtleneck under overalls. She tilts her head when I stop in front of them.

"What're you doing here?" I try to whisper, but it comes out more as an angry hiss.

"Chocolate on a Sunday, sign me up," Andy says. "I had no idea the CIA offered these kinds of classes until yesterday. But having real teachers from the CIA helps a newbie cook like me. Amazing."

"Yeah, except you knew *I* was doing this."

"Well, yeah. It's a class, though," Andy says, gesturing to the room of tables. "A lot of people are doing it. . . . Who is that guy you came in with, by the way? Let me guess . . . Pete?"

I let out a sigh. "Yes, it's Pete."

"So is he your guy?" he asks. For a second, I have to think about what he means by that before I realize he's asking if he's my admirer.

"I don't know," I say.

"You don't seem to know much these days."

"What's that supposed to mean?"

I meet his eyes. It looks like they're searching for something.

"Forget it. If you'd rather we leave, we can," he says. "I was just telling Sarah about the class and we thought it would be a cool experience."

The mention of Sarah makes me stand up straighter. I suddenly realize how ridiculous I must look. Andy said this was a class that anyone could attend. Sure, he was volunteering to leave, but how will it look if I actually take him up on that?

It definitely would give the impression I care.

Do I?

It doesn't seem like he's here to get under my skin. He and Sarah just think it would be a cool experience. But since when do they hang out outside the library? Are they even friends? More importantly, I have to consider Pete. If he sees Andy and Sarah leave after I've been talking to them, he might think there's something going on—and there isn't. The only reason I started hanging out with Andy is because he was willing to drive me places.

And then you started enjoying his company a little too much, I think, but I shove the thought back into my head.

"No! You guys should of course stay. Enjoy!"

"Great," Andy says, giving Sarah a wide smile. They gaze at each other longer than friends would, but then I realize I'm the one staring at the two of them having this moment, which is even weirder. Andy turns back toward me.

"Thanks, Ella," he says casually.

"Er . . . no problem," I say, and head toward the table Pete is stationed at.

I watch Pete's head whip around, like he's been caught spying.

"Friend from the library," I say, taking my place next to him. We share the table with two other couples.

"I've seen that girl before," Pete says, glancing behind us at Sarah. "Aren't you friends with her? I feel like I know her somehow."

I shake my head. "Not really, but she goes to our school."

"Oh," Pete says, but he stares back again confused. I'm glad we're sitting far enough away that he and Andy won't be able to talk.

This class is way more complicated than I imagined it would be. The teacher passes out ingredients I've never heard of and starts demonstrating in front, instructing us to follow along. The organized girl in me wants to be able to take notes, but you can't take notes when your hands are covered with chocolate and everything is on the fly.

I know Pete's a competitive guy when it comes to basketball, but I didn't realize his intensity would also apply to *cooking*. The second the teacher says there will be a contest for the best chocolate ball, he has this look in his eyes like he's going to win. I'm actually glad he's getting into it, because there's no way I'm going to let Andy beat me.

There's a bunch of steps in a row, but once I'm done carefully pouring our bowl into the chocolate mold, I peer over my shoulder to see how Andy and Sarah are doing. I watch Andy scoop his finger into the bowl and then poke Sarah on the nose, getting a spot of chocolate on it. She covers her hand over her mouth to stop herself from laughing. When she turns away to get the chocolate off, he spins her back around and wipes the chocolate right off for her. For a second I think he's going to lick his finger with the chocolate that was on her nose, but thankfully he wipes it off with a towel. Even so, the whole interaction is nauseating.

Why are you even watching them? I ask myself. *Get it together.*

"It's a good thing you're better at basketball than these chocolate balls." I laugh, trying to lighten the mood.

"You're one to talk," he teases. "I'll still give you an A for effort."

"So, uh . . . what are you reading right now?" I ask, resisting the urge to look back at Andy.

"Who has time to read with school?" he answers. "Not to mention I have basketball practice every day."

"Oh right," I say, which could be true, but I notice he doesn't ask what book is on my nightstand right now. There's an awkward pause instead.

"What about for school then?"

"You mean, what am I reading?"

I nod.

"Sparknotes.com." He grins like it's an inside joke between us, but I'm very much on the outside.

I smile, but inside my heart drops. I was really hoping that today would be a game changer for Pete and me. But so far I care more about knowing what Andy's doing than talking to Pete, who is sitting right next to me.

If Pete's my admirer, he's so romantic and kind and all of the things I want in a boyfriend. Shouldn't that count for something? Who cares if he doesn't like to read? That's just one quality about him.

Right, I tell myself. But right now, my heart feels as muddled as the chocolate in front of me.

"Excuse me. I have to use the restroom," I say to Pete. Really, I just need some fresh air. Maybe the heat from the oven is what is making my head feel like it's spinning.

"Okay, but hurry back. We can take the balls out of the freezer in four minutes. Then game time. We can start dipping these suckers."

"Of course . . . ," I say, trailing off.

I really do like how into this chocolate class he is. For some reason, though, I can't be the same. . . .

The second I'm out of the test kitchen, I can breathe again. Still, I go to the bathroom so I can put my hands under cool water. When I see my reflection in the mirror, I'm glad I looked. I quickly reapply my lip gloss and put a little concealer on my cheeks so I don't look so red. I shouldn't have worn such a thick sweater to a cooking class. Once I run my hands under the cool water again, I shake my hands dry before pushing the bathroom door open.

My timing couldn't be worse. There in front of me are Andy and Sarah, standing so close to each other their bodies are practically touching, looking right into each other's eyes. They're definitely more than friends. So much for Andy being jaded.

"Uh, hi, guys," I manage to say.

"Oh, hey," Andy says, grinning at me. Then he turns back to Sarah. "Told you I could find the bathroom." But she's already rushing toward the door. As she passes me, Andy turns his eyes back to me.

"You wouldn't happen to know where the men's bathroom is?"

"Nope," I say. Normally, I'd make a joke about how he's an awful detective, but seeing him and Sarah again like this was surprising. Suddenly, my mouth is all dry.

"So . . . you and . . . ," I start to say, but then I realize it's none of my business. Here I am at a chocolate-making class with another guy, not to mention chasing the paper hearts of a mystery admirer. Obviously, Andy knew I was never interested in him and he was free to do whatever he wanted. But there's still a part of me that feels dumb for thinking there could've been something between us.

"Better get going. Pete wants to start dipping the chocolate balls as soon as they're out of the freezer."

"We're definitely not going to win, so we'll be okay," he laughs.

"Well, it would've helped to keep the chocolate in the pan," I retort.

He raises an eyebrow. I realize I accidentally just admitted I was watching them. "The whole class could hear you two giggling." I shrug, covering up for it.

"We didn't mean to be a distraction," he responds. But when he looks at me now there's a glimmer in his eyes that makes me think that *was* his intention this whole time.

"Oh, I was far from distracted. In fact, I really do think we're going to win."

"Better get going, then," Andy says. "Wouldn't want Paul to have to accept the award alone."

"Pete," I correct him.

"Oh right, I knew that."

He did. Why is he being like this?

"Okay . . . ," I say, walking away slowly. Normally, he would've said at least *one* flirtatious thing by now. What, is he afraid Sarah is going to hear him? I keep walking, and nothing. I don't know what I expect, but the silence is deafening. The only sound is from my boots hitting the floor.

When I'm back at the kitchen, Pete smiles widely. "Just in time!" he says before telling me what I missed while I was in the bathroom. We begin dipping the chocolate balls into the different bowls in front of us, some with nuts, others with sprinkles and more garnishes.

Once everyone is done, the teacher walks around taking

notes to determine the winner. She pauses when she gets to Andy and Sarah, but I force myself to look away before I can see her reaction.

Was the reason I was so bothered about Andy and Sarah because I was jealous? So what if he didn't flirt with me back there? That's all it was before, *flirting*. Not the romantic kind of love I really want.

Right?

Suddenly, I feel Pete nudge my shoulder. The woman in front pulls out three ribbons.

"That blue one is for us," he whispers.

I smile weakly. The third and second place teams are called and then I hear our names as Pete fist-pumps the air next to me. We won.

I glance back at Andy to see if he's watching me, but the chairs he and Sarah were sitting at before are empty. They didn't even bother to stay for the awards. What could they possibly be doing together that's more fun? I turn back to receive the ribbon and Pete's frowning, like he knows why I was looking back.

And even though we're technically winners, I feel like the ultimate loser.

Chapter 18

AFTER THE LONGEST SHOWER OF MY LIFE, I NO LONGER smell like a chocolate bar.

I wrap myself in my fluffiest bathrobe. It's white, and whenever I wear it, I feel like a polar bear, which makes me love it even more.

As I walk to Ashley's room, the faint sound of the music playing from her speakers becomes louder. I knock on her door as drums blare from the other side. I wonder if she can even hear me, so I knock again.

"What?" Ashley yells.

"Can I come in?"

There's a long pause. Then she yells over the music.

"Sure!"

As I enter the room, Ashley's turning the music down. "What's up?" she says from her bed. Her eyes are rimmed with eyeliner but when I join her on the bed, I get a closer view. It looks like they're red underneath, like she's been crying.

I sigh. She was mad at me this morning, but this must not just be about me. I pry gently.

"I came with a peace offering," I say, handing her the bag of chocolates. "Disclaimer, Pete already took two, but it was the least I could give him for leading our team to first place."

"There was a competition?" Ashley says, cracking a smile that also cracks the tension in the room.

"Yes. And you should've seen Pete. He wanted to win so bad like it was a championship game or something. It was *intense.* So know this peace offering was made with blood, sweat, and tears."

I hand the bag to her.

"Want to share one?" she asks. Her hand is already grabbing one out of the bag. She splits the chocolate as evenly as she can, then holds the two pieces out for me to choose from. Our mom taught us this trick when we were young to keep us honest.

I grab the one on the right and pop it into my mouth. Ashley takes a bite and then whips her head toward me.

"Mmm. I *love* the taste of blood."

"Okay, now you sound like a vampire."

"I don't hate that." She smiles. "I'd make a great one."

"A great vampire?"

"Sure," she says, taking another bite and chewing while she

talks. "Instead of going to bed, I could go to concerts all night. You could join me if you want, but you'd probably end up reading from sunset to sunrise."

"I think you're forgetting about the whole biting-other-humans part."

"Small sacrifice."

"Oh boy. Glad I brought a peace offering. You know, to avoid getting my head bitten off."

"I was tempted earlier," she says.

I know this is my opening to take the conversation from vampires to serious sister stuff, so I go for it. "Do you . . . do you want to talk about it?"

"There's not much to talk about," she says, crossing her arms. "You didn't invite me. I was offended. End of story."

"But you never invite me *anywhere*." I don't say it to be mean, only to speak the truth. Deep down I know this has to do with Steve, not me. Right now, Ashley should be listening to her emo music with him, not alone. "Where is Ste—" I start to ask, but she cuts me off.

"We're fighting, okay?"

I knew it. But I can't gloat now.

"About what?"

"Honestly, nothing," she starts. "It's weird. Not that we're picking fights with each other on purpose, but sometimes I get so mad at him and . . ." She trails off.

"You want to bite his head off like a vampire?" I offer.

"Exactly," she says. "It's so frustrating. We never used to fight, and all of a sudden, it happens all the time."

"Do you think you should break up?" I ask. It seems like a perfectly reasonable follow-up question to me, but her jaw drops like I said the most ridiculous thing she's ever heard.

"Couples can fight, Ella. And I don't want to break up with him," Ashley says matter-of-factly. It's the voice she uses when she has heard enough. There's no point in arguing with her now.

"Why?"

"I love him. He's my first real boyfriend. And he's been there for me through so much. After your accident, he was the glue that put me back together."

Ugh. I wish she didn't feel that way.

"What're you thinking?" Ashley asks. "You're so obvious when you're thinking something."

"Nothing."

"You've always been a bad liar." She smiles. "Can't you tell me?"

"I think just because someone is your first love doesn't mean they need to be your last," I say.

"Wise words from someone who hasn't been in love," she says, raising an eyebrow.

I guess everyone at school thought Pete and I were the perfect couple except for my own sister. She sees right through me.

I shrug. "You're right. I can't offer any advice with the way my life is going right now."

"What is that supposed to mean?" she says. "But first have another chocolate ball. It looks like you deserve a whole one." She hands me the one that Pete dipped in red sprinkles. I don't need to be convinced, and I eat the creamy goodness in one bite.

"So delicious," I say. "Okay, fine . . . I guess I just decided I don't like Pete."

"What?!" Ashley gasps. "I was sure that when you invited him, you wanted a second chance."

"I've *tried* to like him. Really, here is this great guy—"

"Who is smart, hot, and likes you even after you stomped on his heart. What more could you want?"

"Gee, thanks, Ashley."

"Sorry. Have another chocolate ball."

I grab one from the bag and eat it before I keep going.

"Well, there's this other guy, Andy, but I don't even know why I'm bringing him up because that's not the problem. I just . . . I know this sounds stupid. But I always thought I'd end up with someone that gave me . . . butterflies."

I spit the last word out, fully knowing that my sister might laugh in my face. After all, she's a self-proclaimed vampire. But she surprises me.

"No, you're right. That's the most important thing."

"Really. You think so?"

"Absolutely."

I can't imagine Steve giving my sister butterflies. Maybe it's more like moths and she's just confused. But I choose not to ruin our sister moment by saying this. Instead, *she's* the one who ruins it.

"So tell me about Andy."

I groan. "Split a chocolate ball with me for this one?"

She breaks one up and lets me choose. I grab the piece closer to me, wondering where to even start. From the beginning? All the paper hearts? No, too much backstory. Instead, I go with what has been eating me up inside.

"He came to the chocolate-making class with another girl even though he knew I was going to be there."

"That's so rude!" Ashley says. "Who's the girl?"

"Her name is Sarah. They work together at the library."

"Oh, so maybe it's not what you think," she says, taking a bite of the chocolate.

"No, it is. The way they were looking at each other. They were more interested in flirting with each other than making chocolates. I don't even know why they went."

"Sounds like he was trying to make you jealous."

"*Jealous?*" I spit.

"It also sounds like it worked."

"Did not!" I say loudly. Too loudly. Ashley looks at me with a big smirk on her face. "He can go on chocolate dates with anyone he wants to," I continue. "He isn't my boyfriend. We're just friends."

"Friends who have been spending an awful lot of time to-gether, judging by the fact that I haven't seen you locked in your room for days."

"Yeah, we have," I admit. "And I thought we were having a lot of fun."

"Have you told him that?" Ashley asks.

"Well, no . . . ," I start.

"It's pretty obvious you should have a conversation with him," Ashley says.

"Why?"

"I don't know, it's good to see you like this."

"Like what?"

"Like your old self again," she says, like it's obvious.

"You mean before the accident? Finally."

"No," she says, looking up at me. "I mean even before that. Before, when we were close."

"Ouch," I retort.

"You know it's true."

"Well, maybe that's why that hurt."

Ashley nods. "Yeah, I wish we were closer now too."

"Really?" I ask, surprised.

"Yeah. We used to tell each other everything, but once you got to high school . . . I don't know, I think I always feel second choice to your friends."

My eyes widen. "Aw, Ash, that's so not true."

"I mean, I get it. I'm younger than you, and—"

"No," I say, cutting her off. "I don't want you to ever feel that way. What can I do?"

"Maybe the next time we're hanging out, can you not ditch your only sister? Deal?"

I smile. "Deal."

She hands me the bag of chocolates. I reach inside, searching for one of the remaining pieces, when my fingertips feel something else—paper.

I look inside and see it: another paper heart.

Oh my God. How on earth did that get in there? I think, but Ashley doesn't seem to notice. Suddenly, there's a loud chime from the doorbell.

"That's been ringing a lot lately." Ashley smiles.

"Yeah, well, it's not for me this time," I say confidently. Neither Pete nor Andy would want to see me after that fiasco.

"I'll get it since you're in your robe," she says, getting up and leaving me alone on her bed. As she heads downstairs, I debate opening the paper heart while she's gone, until I hear Ashley shout.

"Ella, it's for you!"

"Coming!" I yell back right away, but I'm startled. Who could it possibly be?

I rush to my room and throw on the first yoga pants and T-shirt I can find. When I make my way down the stairs, I see Pete standing at the doorway. He's not smiling like he was the times he greeted me for our past two dates. In fact, he looks like I think he would've looked if we'd lost that chocolate competition. This can't be good.

"What's up?" I ask. As I do, Ashley disappears into the other room.

Pete shifts uncomfortably. "I was going to text you, but you and I both know that you're not the best responder."

Ouch.

"That's not fair—" I start, but I'm cut off.

"I didn't come here to argue. I just came here to find out why."

"Why what?"

He looks down at his sneakers for a second, then back up at me. "Why you never look at me like you looked at Andy today. I may use Sparknotes, but I'm not dumb, Ella. I . . . just . . . I just want to know why."

I sigh. Of course he wants to know why. He's Pete Yearling. He always gets what he wants. But now the one thing he wants is me, and even I don't know why I don't want him back. So that's what I tell him.

"I don't know," I start to say. "It's not you at all. It's me and all the stupid thoughts that go in my head. When we're together, all I can think about is why I'm not happier. You're so sweet and so perfect, but I just . . . can't bring myself to feel—"

"The same way that I feel about you."

I pause. "How did you know I was going to say that?"

For a moment, there are tears shining in his eyes, but he

brushes them away. "Because that's exactly what you told me before the accident. Right before you told me your heart just wasn't in it."

"I'm sorry," I say, because there's nothing else I can say.

He shakes his head. "You don't have to be. . . . I should go. Sorry for bothering you."

"You don't have to be," I say, repeating his words.

The tears in his eyes are back and I feel like I should hug him or something, but he quickly turns and heads out the door. As it shuts, Ashley returns to the room. I can't tell if she's been listening the whole time. Before I can ask, she looks at me. "Now there's someone else you need to talk to."

~

We drive to the library, my unopened paper heart tucked into my jean pocket. Whether it's from Pete or someone else doesn't seem to matter now. What matters is talking to Andy.

But what exactly am I going to say?

Obviously, that I enjoyed spending time with him, but what else? If he's already talking to Sarah, it won't matter. It'll be too late. Andy and Sarah actually have stuff in common. They both work at the library, love books, and more than that, love being right. They wouldn't exactly be a random couple. Maybe they'd even be a good one. I sigh.

Why was I even going to go talk to him, again?

"We should turn around," I say to Ashley in the driver seat.

"Why?" she snaps.

"Because I want to. And you have to listen to me. I don't question your decisions with Steve."

"See, you always bring Steve into it," Ashley says, rolling her eyes. "I'm not getting into it but if you don't go to the library, you're a big baby."

"I'm fine with that," I say automatically. "Besides, aren't you supposed to fall in love, not chase it?"

"You're not chasing him. You're telling him that you enjoy spending time with him in case there was some sort of misunderstanding."

I take in a deep breath. "Okay. I can do that."

"Of course you can."

"Of course I can," I repeat, but I know I don't believe it. "Maybe I can just ask him to go on my next paper heart hunt with me?" I ask as we're pulling into the library parking lot.

"That's not a bad idea," Ashley says. "If he says no, you'll have your answer."

I gulp. She's right. If Andy says no, it means he and Sarah are practically dating and he feels guilty. Or even worse, he has no real reason and just doesn't want to.

It would hurt either way.

"You've got this," Ashley says.

I'm not so sure. All I've got is some major things happening to my stomach . . . and it's not butterflies. Why am I so nervous? I shake my head. I just have to play it cool. For all he knows, I'm still totally invested in these paper hearts.

"A hug for good luck," Ashley says, grabbing me and pulling me into her big puffer jacket. It makes me smile. My mom used to do that on mornings when we missed our bus and had to get dropped off at school. Normally, it was because something stressful had happened to ruin the morning routine—one of us had forgotten to do our homework or spilled OJ all over our clothes, or some other equally chaotic mess-up. Mom always knew when I was already feeling frazzled to take a deep breath and give me a tight little hug. It lasted only a few seconds, but it always stopped time for me, and her squeezing me would squeeze out all my stress.

Now I realize that Ashley inherited that talent. When she releases me, I'm ready to take on the world, or at least walk into the library without crumbling.

I slide out of the car and make my way to the door quickly before I lose my confidence again.

But when I walk inside, I'm instantly deflated, because I forgot the one worst possible thing that could happen.

Sarah's alone at the front desk.

My instinct is to run back to the car, but she looks up and waves. I almost have to do a double take. Is she really waving at me? I guess going to the same cooking class makes us friends now, or at least classmates that say hi.

I reluctantly walk over to her. After all, it's not her fault if Andy likes her.

"Hey," I say when I reach the desk. "Is Andy around?"

"No, I haven't seen him," she starts to say. "He should be here soon to start his shift. Want me to text him?"

"No, that's okay!" I say quickly. "I was just wondering. I'm going to browse a little. Did you have fun at the class?" I ask. Hopefully, I can stomach the answer.

"Yes! It was so much fun. But Andy can make anything fun, ya know?"

"Yeah, I do," I say. *That's what I came here to tell him, but you said it better than me.* "It looked like you two were really hitting it off."

I cringe at that last part. It came off way more jealous than I intended. But Sarah doesn't seem to notice.

"Yeah, I'm so glad he invited me."

You can't be mad, Ella, I think. *You could've invited him and you didn't.*

"Did you have fun?" she asks me now. "Oh, and did you guys end up winning? You put our chocolate balls to shame."

Her voice is genuine. It makes me wonder why.

"Sarah, can I ask you why you're nice to me? My friends are such jerks to you."

She shrugs. "You're not."

"Yeah, but . . . I should make them stop."

231

She looks at me thoughtfully. "People change, but you can't change people."

I nod like I understand, but really, I *don't understand* how Sarah can be so forgiving.

"But . . ." I trail off.

"I get it—really. I've had friends like Carmen. Maybe not quite so . . . *intense,*" she says, making me laugh. "But once I let them go, I found that being myself was never so easy."

"Really? I can't imagine you struggling with that."

I think back to the paper heart I wrote to her. How I love the way she dresses with her own style, not the typical ensemble you'd see on Instagram. How she answers all the questions in English because she loves books and she doesn't care if people think she's a know-it-all. It really is hard to believe there was a time when she wasn't like that.

"I mean, that was freshman year. Plenty of confidence boosting had to happen. Oh, and I discovered Mary Oliver—she got me through some stuff. You should check her out sometime."

" 'Tell me, what is it you plan to do with your one wild and precious life?' " I say, quoting one of her poems. It's one of my favorite quotes; I have it in a frame above the desk in my bedroom. I've also written it in my notebook more than I'd like to admit.

She smiles. "See? You don't need my advice when you have Mary."

"Well, thank you anyway. Really."

"Don't mention it," she says, turning to the computer on her desk. I spin around, heading toward the romance section of the library. I can't help but feel like I should just leave.

If Sarah were mean to me, I could think that Andy deserves better. But if she's actually nice and can talk books with him and the two of them have fun together, then . . .

But I don't get to finish my thought, because in walks Andy. Through the space in the bookshelves I can see him saunter over to the front desk. I brace myself for Andy to do something flirty with Sarah. Maybe hug her when he sees her, or something worse. But when he reaches her, she says something to him and he spins around in my direction. It's not like I'm trying to hide, but I instinctively duck lower so he can't see me behind the shelf. I stand there crouched all frozen, hoping he didn't see me watching them. How embarrassing would that be?

But moments later I hear a voice.

"Ella?"

It's Andy. Now, this is *more* than embarrassing. I want to unlock my legs and look at him like a normal human but they seem to have stopped working. I grab a random book in front of me.

"Oh, here it is!" I say, before I will my legs to let me stand. When I turn to Andy, he has a big stupid grin on his face.

"Why were you looking for *Losing It in Paris*?"

"I've heard great things," I say, totally lying.

"Oh, interesting. I wonder how it compares to *Fifty Shades of Grey.*"

"Why do you wonder that . . . ," I start, but I look down at the cover. This book is clearly erotica. And instantly, I turn fifty shades of red.

"Sarah said you were looking for me," Andy says.

"Mm," I barely get out. "Not to help me find this, of course. I actually think I got the title wrong," I add, placing the book back on the shelf. God, why am I so nervous? This is just Andy. The boy who can be utterly flirtatious and funny. Not to mention understanding. I just picked up an erotica book and he didn't laugh in my face.

Andy grins now, with his smile that gets me every time. "Well, did you need help with something else?"

I feel like melting, but luckily, I think quickly and reach into my back pocket to pull out the paper heart, then hand it to him.

"You're giving this to me because . . . ?" he says before reading it.

"What does it say, Sherlock? I was hoping we could do this next one together."

He pauses. After a couple of seconds, he hands it back.

"I can't do that," he says.

"Can't or won't?" I say. I'm surprised I can say anything at all. My heart feels like it has shattered into a million pieces.

"Can't and won't. First of all, I'm working. Second of all, I want you to find what you're looking for, but . . . this isn't my mystery to solve."

His words make me want to crawl underneath the bookshelf. Why did I come here?

Andy's right. This isn't his mystery to solve, but I'm the one standing here asking him. Since he doesn't want to help me, he clearly doesn't want to be with me either. This stings like a paper cut.

But I'm not about to let him see that I care. I shrug like his answer is no big deal and plaster a fake smile on my face. "Oh, that's okay. I should've known you can't leave work. I'll get out of your way."

His mouth opens like he's going to say something, but then he snaps it shut, lost for words. *That's* a first. But it doesn't even matter. He already said what he needed to.

"I'll see you around," I say, stepping past him.

"Ella," he calls to me, but I'm already headed for the exit. I feel him following me until we reach the front of the library. He veers straight toward Sarah.

It already felt like my heart fell out of my chest, but watching him go off to another girl makes it feel like Andy's straight-up stomping on it. I will myself not to cry—not yet, anyway. I have too much pride. I take a deep breath and continue walking toward the door, blocking out the fact that I asked Andy to do something with me and he went running to another girl.

Why did I even put myself in this position? I thought I could handle it, but the way my world is spinning right now shows me I can't.

Just as I reach the door, I hear Andy behind me.

"Forget everything I said back there."

"I may have retrograde amnesia but I'm pretty sure I won't be able to forget that," I say bitterly.

Andy smiles. "Well, try. Sarah said she'd cover for me."

"I thought you said this isn't your mystery to solve?"

"It isn't. But it would be my privilege to join you."

Chapter 19

WE WALK TO AN OLD MOVIE THEATER AT THE EDGE OF town, our hands so close they're almost touching. I have the urge to grab his hand but resist and reach into my pocket for the paper heart instead.

A story in front of your eyes
Show these tickets at the entrance.

"You said this was it," Andy says, watching me skim the note.

"It is. I'm just double-checking."

"What, you think the message is going to change?" He grins at me.

"Like I said, I was just double-checking. I want to make sure

I'm not leading us to the wrong place. I've done that enough times."

He grabs my shoulders and stops me in my tracks. He looks down at me and for a second I think he's stopping to kiss me. But he doesn't lean over and his lips curl into a smirk.

"Um. What're we doing?" I ask.

"I'm just double-checking I'm with the right girl. About five feet two. Blond. Probably has emergency heart-shaped snacks in her purse."

"Very funny. Let's go," I say, walking ahead of him.

"Slightly demanding," he calls out. "Oh, and a fast walker too!"

I smile but my back is toward him as I keep walking, so he can't see the stupid grin on my face. Soon he catches up and passes me to beat me to the entrance. He opens the door for me, a cage of butterflies in my stomach opening with it.

At the box office there's a girl around our age working. I recognize her from somewhere but I can't put my finger on it. Her name tag says SAMANTHA, which seems familiar. Maybe she's in my sister's year at school.

I slide her the tickets that were in my paper heart, hoping she doesn't laugh in my face. When she sees them, her eyes light up.

"Last theater on your right," Samantha says. "It may take a moment to set up, so take your time getting comfortable."

It reminds me of the time I got my nails done at the spa and the woman behind the front desk was expecting me.

"Whoa, we need to make a pit stop first," Andy says. "Are you a popcorn or candy kind of girl?"

"Hmm . . ."

"Wrong answer," he says.

"I didn't give an answer."

"It was a trick question. I'm getting both so we can put M&Ms in our popcorn. Duh."

"That seems excessive even for you."

"Are you joking? It's the perfect combination of salty and sweet. You've never tried it?"

I shake my head.

"Well, I'd be happy to be your first."

For a second I think he's saying something else, and I can feel my cheeks burn. Andy doesn't notice, though. He turns and orders the popcorn and M&Ms and one soda.

"You're okay sharing, right?" he asks.

"I'm actually worried about your cooties," I say sarcastically.

"Guess I won't be kissing you after this date, then," he says. His lips are pursed like he's trying not to smile. "Oh, I forgot this isn't a date," he adds as the man behind the counter brings his order.

Andy grabs the popcorn and soda.

"Sure feels like a date," I say, heading to the theater before I can see his reaction. I don't have to see him to know his dimple is showing.

When we reach the theater, I see a sign that says PRIVATE PARTY on the outside. My jaw drops. It's going to be just me and Andy?

Andy's jaw drops too, but for a different reason.

"I forgot the M&Ms."

"Good" is all I say.

"No way. I need you to experience the sweet and salty excessiveness."

I laugh. "If you say so."

"I do. Go in and enjoy the previews. I'll be right back."

Again, I have the urge to kiss Andy. A boy who will go back and stand in line so I can try something he likes for the first time. I enter the theater smiling widely, feeling like I've been transported back a hundred years. The dim lighting makes it feel like I'm looking at a blurry black-and-white photo, with old pictures flickering on the screen. The seats are also the plush vintage kind, not like the collapsible ones at the mall theater.

Where do you sit when you have an entire theater to yourself? Dead center, of course. I count the seats in each row and the total number of rows. I make my way to the middle, but as soon as I put the soda in my armrest, I start to worry that I'll ruin the whole thing mid-movie by having to get up to use the restroom.

I make my way out of the theater, following the signs that

take me toward the front again. As I'm walking, Samantha from the box office walks by in a hurry, texting something frantically on her phone. It suddenly comes to me how I recognize her. My mom has a program at her practice where high school students can follow the different doctors for the summer. Samantha was her "shadow." There's a picture of the two of them in the *Poughkeepsie Journal.*

And suddenly the idea pops into my head like a popcorn kernel in a microwave.

What if Samantha was the one who set this whole thing up?

Before I have time to decide if that's right, I dart into the bathroom. Then I look in the mirror at my reflection and gasp at everything coming together.

I know who my admirer could be.

It's my mom.

The truth seems so obvious now. Why haven't I figured this out yet? She's the one who wants me to get back out there, and she knows me better than practically anyone. Of course it's her!

Any guilt I had before about possibly falling for Andy while some other admirer was sending me paper hearts washes away, and I can finally admit the truth to myself: I'm falling for everything about Andy. His face. His dimple. His humor. His mind. Him.

And for once, I'm grateful for something I didn't plan.

I return to the theater and Andy has found our seats in the middle where I left my coat. I sit down next to him and this time I don't resist the urge to grab his hand. His eyes widen for a second but he squeezes mine back and then lets go, only to put his arm around me. I breathe in his cologne and rest my head on his shoulder, eating popcorn with chocolate, which ends up being more delicious than I expected. Each bite melts in my mouth.

When the lights go down, it suddenly feels like we're slipping into an actual dream. The movie starts with the opening credits of *Pride and Prejudice*. My favorite. I've seen it plenty of times, but never with Andy. I feel his chest move every time he laughs or his heart speeds up.

When the movie ends, the credits start rolling and I finally lift my head off his shoulder. He grabs my hand and leads me to the aisle. I think we're leaving, but he stops me before putting his hand on my lower back.

"What're you doing?" I ask.

"Be spontaneous with me," he whispers in my ear. "Dance with me in an empty movie theater. It's kind of like a fantasy for me. I hope you don't mind."

"I think it's one of mine too, but I didn't know until just this second," I say, smiling.

We sway back and forth to the music as the projector shines down from above, making me completely breathless. Before the song ends, he dips me like you see in the movies and gives me the most utterly perfect first kiss I could ever imagine.

~

Andy pretends to get lost as he drives me home so we can have more time together. It becomes a running joke and he keeps making wrong turns, both of us laughing more than we should each time he does it. At one point we have to stop for gas and he comes back to the car with more snacks than the two of us can eat. Once we hit the road, Andy gets "lost" again. I tell him the joke's going to grow tired, and he just looks at me and says we'll never grow tired of each other. It's only after he says it that I realize we're driving by the bridge where we had our first unofficial date. They say time flies when you're having fun, but I have a feeling the memory of today will last forever.

When I get home, my mom's at the kitchen table like she always is when she's waiting up for me. She pretends she isn't, though, reading some medical journal. I kiss her on the cheek before heading upstairs and not giving away that I'm on to her.

Chapter 20

I'M STILL ON CLOUD NINE ON MONDAY AND IT FEELS LIKE nothing can bring me down, even the fact that nobody has been able to stop talking about the Valentine's Day Dance.

"So who do you think is going to ask you?" Katie asks Jess at lunch. My group of friends always sits at the table closest to the window. There's no assigned seating, but tables are pretty much declared early on. Carmen got to the cafeteria early the first day to snag the best one, since, according to her, she wasn't going to leave one of the most crucial elements of our senior year up to chance. Just like she's not going to leave Jess's date up to chance now.

"I'll tell Anthony to get Connor to ask you," she declares.

"Isn't he dating that girl Lizzie?" she asks.

"No, they're dunzo."

Katie plays with the bracelet on her wrist. It's what she does when she disagrees with what Carmen's saying.

"What?" Carmen demands. Clearly, she has picked up on this habit too.

Jess shakes her head. "I just don't know if Connor would want to go with me."

Carmen smiles. "Of course he will. Anthony is going with me and Pete's going with Ella. Now we just need Connor to go with you and find someone for Katie." She turns to her now. "What do you think of James?"

"You suggest Connor for Jess and *James* for me? Rude."

"Not everyone can go with Pete Yearling," Carmen says, winking at me.

I let it go the first time, but I know I need to correct it now.

"I'm not going with Pete," I say.

Carmen shakes her head. "You've been going on actual dates with him. He's obviously going to ask you to the dance too. He's not a moron."

For a moment, I glance at Pete across the cafeteria. He's eating a sandwich while his buddy Vince is telling him some sort of story, waving his arms in excitement. Pete nods. Maybe it's just because he's between bites, but he's not smiling, the way he normally is. I hope he's not still bummed about us. Just because he's not a great guy for me doesn't mean he won't be a great guy for someone else.

"No, I'm actually not going with Pete," I say again, looking down at the table. "We ended it . . . whatever *it* was."

"What happened?" Carmen exclaims. "I thought everything was going great. . . ."

"It was. I just wasn't into him."

Carmen's eyes widen. "You're telling me *you* ended things *again*." Katie and Jessica give each other looks. I can feel my cheeks burning.

"Yes," I answer. "But he knew something wasn't right. He was the one who brought it up."

Carmen nods like she's trying to understand, but there's a hint of anger in her eyes, like the time some new girl tried to sit at our lunch table after winter break.

"So who do you plan on going with *now*?" she asks.

"I don't know." I shrug. "I haven't really thought about it."

That's the truth. Besides, the only person I'd really want to go with is Andy, and he's not allowed to come. Dances are for Arlington High students only. But Carmen continues to glare at me so I offer a new suggestion.

"Maybe we can just go as us girls. I think we'd have way more fun anyway."

Katie and Jess's eyes light up but Carmen laughs.

"Girls like us don't need to act like going without boys will be more fun. That's just what girls who can't get guys say to make themselves feel better," Carmen says. "Hard pass for me."

Katie plays with the bracelet on her wrist again before she realizes what she's doing.

"What, Katie?" Carmen snaps.

"Nothing," she says, her hands flying underneath the table. "Ella's idea just sounded like it could be fun," she says in a whisper.

Then Jess comes to her rescue. "Plus, I'd rather go with each other than some rando just to have a date."

She looks at me to chime in too.

But I hesitate. The anger in Carmen's eyes has changed to pure shock. "You can still go with Anthony, obviously," I say. "I just don't think I want to go with any of his friends. And besides, we're all going to dance with each other. The date is really just for the pictures beforehand—"

"You mean the most important part," Carmen interrupts.

"Debatable," I say, but I don't actually want to have that argument right now.

Suddenly, I'm relieved that Andy doesn't go to the same school as us. I'm sure if I wanted to go with him, Carmen would be having an even bigger fit right now. I remember how she called him a nerd that one time she saw him in the library. She shakes her head at me now in the same disgusted way she did when she saw us together.

"I was just looking out for my best friends," Carmen says. "Don't come crying to me when the three of you change your minds and the good dates are all taken," she says.

I give her a small smile to ease the tension of the table. "We won't."

But I regret it immediately when Carmen squints at me while pursing her lips—she's going to snap.

"I'm surprised you don't want to go with anyone, considering."

I take the bait. "Considering what?"

"I don't know. All of this is starting to feel a little like déjà vu. You didn't have a date last year and left early for a reason."

"Carmen," Jess snaps as I see Katie moving her hands rapidly underneath the table. "You did *not* just say that."

"I wasn't implying that something bad is going to happen. I'm just saying it's a weird coincidence," Carmen says, turning from her to me, eyes flashing. "Don't you think?"

"I didn't put two and two together," I say back.

But now that I am, I can't help but think of Sydney at the nail salon. How I found out Carmen and I weren't together like always right before the dance. Carmen said it was because I was being a bad friend, but at this second, I'm finding that hard to believe. "Is this why you were mad at me last year too?" I ask. "Because I didn't go with Pete?"

Jess and Katie look at each other nervously.

"How did you know I was mad at you before the dance?" Carmen asks. "I never told you that. Did either of you?" Carmen asks, turning to Katie and Jess. They shake their heads.

"Why are you avoiding the question?" I ask in disbelief. What was she trying to hide that from me for?

"No, I wasn't just mad at you because you didn't have a date."

Just? So that was part of the reason. Are you kidding me? What was the other? My face must show my anger, though, because Carmen gets defensive.

"Don't turn this on me," she says. "This was literally a year ago—not my fault you can't remember."

It's not just what she says but how she says it that makes me stand up at the table. Jess flinches as my chair screeches on the cafeteria floor.

"You're right," I say. "It doesn't matter why I was mad at you last year. Just that I'm furious with you right now."

Then I walk away from the table that Carmen so carefully chose for us. Her mouth is now fully open. Maybe this was déjà vu for Carmen, but it's the first time I'm standing up to her and her impossible standards . . . and it feels good.

Chapter 21

I NEVER IMAGINED GOING TO THE VALENTINE'S DAY DANCE with my sister and Skeevy Stevey, but there have been crazier things that have happened to me.

I text Andy a selfie after I'm dressed. A lot of girls will be wearing red or hot pink dresses, but I choose a black halter that hides the scar on my collarbone. I love it, and I smile when I hit send.

Andy texts back a series of emojis with a simple message that makes my heart jump.

Wow. You look beautiful.

We've been texting a lot lately—so much that I haven't minded the fact that I haven't received a paper heart in over a week. Andy is always full of sweet things to say, but this one in particular makes me smile. I type back.

That's just a preview. My parents will be taking photos of
me and Ashley before we go pick up Steve.

Good call. That way you won't have to crop Steve out when
they break up.

I laugh as I read it, because at the same time, I hear Ashley
whining my name from the bathroom.

Fair point. I'll text you more pics soon.

When I head to the bathroom my jaw drops. This is the first
time I've seen Ashley in a color other than black in months.
She's wearing a red strapless dress and matching red lipstick,
but her mouth is currently in a pout.

"What's wrong? You look great," I say.

"You don't need to lie to me," she says dramatically. "Of
course I would have a bad hair day today of all days."

"What're you talking about?" She has curled her hair, which
is a nice change since normally it's pin-straight.

"Are you sure? I can't see the back, and I feel like I missed
some pieces." She turns around and I see that she's not wrong.
I grab the hot iron from the bathroom counter. "Let me help,"
I say. She stands still as I loop the first strand around the metal
clamp.

"Why are you so much better at this than me?" she whines.

"A lot of practice," I laugh. "Remember how me and Carmen would wear gloves when we first started because we kept

burning ourselves?" I stop, realizing Jess or Katie is probably doing her hair right now.

Ashley gives me a small smile in the mirror. "Do you want to talk about what happened?"

"What do you mean?"

Ashley raises an eyebrow. "I'm really happy that you want to third-wheel with me and Steve, but I know that's not exactly your first choice. Obviously, something happened. Is Carmen mad at you again?"

I nod. "I'm always disappointing her in one way or another. She wants me to be something and I just don't."

"Have you tried saying that to her?" Ashley asks.

I wrap another piece of hair around the barrel of the iron. "Well, no," I admit.

"I think maybe you should. You guys are too good of friends to not talk it out, and if she doesn't want to hear it . . . you don't need a friend like that."

I nod. "Giving your older sister advice. Who are you these days?"

Ashley smiles.

"Do you think it's going to be weird for you tonight . . . you know, going to the dance, since last year . . ." She trails off.

I spin her around to face me. I remember Ashley when she was a little girl with skinned knees, applesauce in her pigtails, and colored marker all over her hands. But tonight, I'll remember her looking absolutely beautiful.

252

"Yes, tonight is weird for me, but that's why this is important. I don't want it to be. That's why I'm doing this even though all my friends are going to the dance without me. When I think of the Valentine's Day Dance, I want to have new memories . . . so no pressure, but we *have* to have fun tonight."

"We can do that." She smiles. Then she squeezes my hand three times like she used to do.

~

The gym looks like it's been hit with Cupid's arrow. The walls and ceiling are covered in pink twinkling lights. The planner in me starts looking around, making a checklist of all the things I would've done differently, like put the flower wall on the far end of the gymnasium so the line doesn't block the entrance as people come in. But it looks beautiful, and I feel a twinge of sadness, knowing that I had nothing to do with it.

The DJ has started playing music, but nobody wants to be first on the dance floor. On the far side of the basketball court is a flower wall donated by the florist next door. There's a line for pictures.

"Oooh! We need one together," Ashley says to Steve, grabbing his arm. He's wearing a black suit with black Converses that actually look pretty good together. But as she turns with me we see Carmen and the rest of my friends get in the back of the line. They're all wearing minidresses in shades of pink,

with stilettos. I wonder if Carmen recruited one of them to get their nails done together.

Ashley follows the direction of my eyes. "Never mind. Let's wait until the line isn't as long."

"Good idea."

We turn around, and walking in with his date is Pete. The girl named Molly who he was apparently seeing before me has her arm locked in his. She's wearing a red dress with mesh cutouts.

Stop staring, I tell myself. But it's too late. Suddenly, I've locked eyes with Pete across the gym. He gives me a small smile, which in a way is comforting. We're back to being exes. I just wish I could've come here with Andy. If I had, it wouldn't matter that I'm not talking to any of my friends. Luckily, I have Ashley.

"Maybe we won't run into anyone by the punch," she suggests now, but as she says it Steve's head jerks toward the DJ, who has started playing a slow song.

"I love this song!" Steve says. "Let's dance."

Ashley looks at the dance floor. "Nobody else is dancing yet."

He shrugs. "So we'll be the first."

The way Ashley smiles lets me know this is the most romantic thing he's ever said. She looks at me.

"Go!" I encourage her. "I have to go to the bathroom anyway."

"Are you sure?"

I smile. "Yes, I'll come third wheel after."

"Okay!" she says. As Steve whisks her away to the dance floor, she turns around to mouth *thank you.*

I head to the bathroom, passing the punch table on the way. There's a little sign that says LOVE POTION that makes me smile. It's clever—I bet Sarah came up with it.

I'm relieved when I get to the bathroom. It's early enough that there's not a long line yet, and anybody that's willing to stand in a long line is trying to get the first pictures at the flower wall. I take the opportunity to do a quick lipstick fix in the mirror. By the end of the dance it'll be impossible to do.

As I'm putting my lipstick back in my bag, I hear familiar voices outside the bathroom door.

"I still can't believe we got booed trying to cut the line."

It's Jess. *Of course they tried to cut the line,* I think as I sprint to the nearest stall.

"I said we shouldn't do it," I hear Katie say as the bathroom door opens. "You and Carmen insisted."

From underneath the stall door I watch their heels head toward the bathroom mirror. If they see my nude heels, they don't care because they keep talking.

"Yeah, well, now she's mad like it's all our fault," Jess says.

"She'll get over it. She's just embarrassed Anthony was watching when it happened."

"Does Carmen get over anything?" Her voice lowers. "She's *still* mad about what Ella did last year. It's obvious."

What I did last year? What did I do?

"It's also low-key hilarious that history is repeating itself. It's like Carmen said. Freaking déjà vu. But Carmen better be careful. Pretty soon someone is going to tell Ella why she stopped being friends with us last year and became attached at the hip to that rando."

My head starts to spin.

"Carmen would kill them. Everyone knows that. She's never been meaner than when Ella ditched her for Sarah Chang."

Ditched her for Sarah Chang? It takes everything in me to stop myself from gasping.

"In Ella's defense, I don't blame her," Katie says. "Carmen's so controlling. Who Ella is friends with. Who Ella dates. I mean, it still blows my mind that Ella broke up with Pete for that guy, but that's beside the point."

My head is spinning. I broke up with Pete for someone else? Is this who Sydney thought I was in love with? But if I was in love with someone, why would they have just disappeared after the accident? Why is everyone hiding him from me?

"But Carmen better chill. She's obviously still racked with guilt for what she did last year. Why else is she shipping them so hard?"

"I don't know why she hasn't just told Ella yet. Carmen

should just say the truth—'you and Pete were broken up and the five minutes behind the flower wall wasn't worth losing my friendship with you but I messed up.'"

"Do you think Ella would forgive her?"

"Probably. You know she's kind of a pushover with Carmen."

With that last remark, I can no longer bite my tongue. I swing open the stall door. Behind Jess and Katie, I see my reflection staring back at me in the mirror. There's a look of determination on my face. I'm ready to demand answers.

"Who did I break up with Pete for?" I ask. I don't even care that Carmen kissed Pete at this point, now that I know there's something even bigger they're keeping from me. My voice sounds angry because I am. All this time my friends knew things that I didn't and they chose to keep them hidden from me. So much for always having each other's backs. Both Katie's and Jess's mouths drop like they've seen a ghost. "Tell me," I say, raising my voice this time.

They're silent. I stare at them, waiting for them to say something—anything—when the bathroom door *whish*es open. It's Carmen, of all people. She widens her eyes at me, but then she looks at Jess and Katie, who still look like deer caught in headlights.

"What's wrong?" she asks.

"Nothing," I answer for them. "They were just about to tell me why I broke up with Pete last year."

She whips her head at them and that's all I need to know. She knew too.

"Oh, and this was after they already said that you made out with Pete."

Her cheeks flame in a way I haven't seen before, even brighter than her dress. She's completely guilty.

"You three disgust me," I say, my voice seething. "All this time you watched me struggle with losing my memories and you decide to keep them from me. For what? So you can keep this fake image going that we're best friends? Because you care so much what other people think? What about *me*?"

"Calm down," Carmen says, grabbing my arms. "Let me explain."

I rip myself away from her.

"Explain what? Explain that you're a terrible friend?" Then I say the one thing that I know will hurt her the most. "No wonder I ditched you for Sarah Chang."

She looks at me angrily, like she wants to slap me. But the damage is done. It feels like the one thread holding our best friend bracelet together has snapped. "Do you know how good a friend I've been to you this whole year? *Poor me. I was in an accident and I can't remember it.* Do you know how annoying that's been? I mean, really. Who knew you'd have a pity party for yourself that long? Meanwhile, we knew that accident was the best thing that ever happened to you. Before it happened, you were throwing everything good out of your life. Pete. Me.

But please tell me how bad a friend I am again. There won't be another accident for you to get a third chance."

I stare at her in disbelief. It feels like the pieces of our friendship are scattered on the floor and I can't pick them up to put it back together. Or admit it that if I try to put it back together, it's only going to break again.

"I don't want another chance," I finally say. "I want to remember walking away from you."

I storm out of the bathroom, wiping my eyes. Ashley's at the edge of the dance floor with Steve because some pop song is on. She smiles when she sees me and waves me over. It's only as I get closer and she can see the anger on my face that her smile fades.

"What's wrong?" she asks.

I want to tell her everything. I want to ask her what she knew too. But I'm so angry I can't bear to be mad at her too.

"Give me your keys," I say.

She grabs my shoulders. "*You're* going to drive? Are you feeling okay?" she asks.

All I do is nod.

"Where are you going?" she asks, reaching into her silver clutch. She pulls out her keys and I grab them before she changes her mind.

"Tell Mom I'm sleeping at Katie's or something."

At this moment it feels like I'm never going to talk to her again, but my mom doesn't know that.

"Where are you actually going?" Ashley asks, but I don't even know the answer to that. All I know is I need to get away—away from everyone who has been lying to me.

I storm out of the dance like I stormed out of the bathroom, only stopping at the flower wall to interrupt Sarah Chang, who is getting her picture taken.

The photographer looks at me, annoyed. "Can't you see there's a line?" he asks, gesturing toward the one wrapping outside.

"One second," I snap back.

Sarah's eyes are wide when I turn back. "Are you okay?" she asks. I wonder if she can see the tears that are still floating in my eyes.

"I just want to say I don't remember, but I found out we were friends. I don't know why you didn't want to tell me. You know what? It's okay. We should talk. Just not now. I'm heading out. Enjoy the dance," I say, leaving her with her mouth wide open as the photographer takes her photo.

~

Before I know it, I'm out in the parking lot, searching for the car, my heels clacking loudly on the pavement. It's freezing, and of course I'm coatless because I didn't want to worry about it at the dance, so I'm walking around the empty parking lot with my arms and legs exposed to the cold air. I feel little goose

bumps on my skin, fully raised. They only rise higher when I reach my car because there's a voice behind me.

"Ella, please don't leave me."

I know it's Carmen before I spin around. Once I do, she continues.

"Can we please just talk about this?"

"Talk about what, Carmen? How you made out with my ex-boyfriend? Or worse, how you've been lying to me about everything for a full year?"

Just when I think I can't be any madder at her, she reaches into her clutch and pulls out a paper heart. My mouth drops.

"I've been thinking a lot since our fight. . . . I was planning on giving this to you tonight."

"How long have you had that?" I ask. It's my tenth paper heart. I've been so close to the end and she's been keeping it from me, just like she's kept everything else.

"Since Tuesday when I found it in your lock—"

"So you stole from me too? Great. How am I supposed to ever trust you again, Carmen?"

She looks down at her heels. "I don't know."

All I can do is shake my head. Here she is again, playing the victim. I find the right key on the key chain and start opening the door.

"Wait, Ellie. Please. You're right. I've been a bad friend. I should've told you about Pete, but I . . . I was so hurt that you were becoming better friends with Sarah than me. It felt like you just left me . . . and I was crushed. The kiss didn't mean anything. I felt so guilty, but that's why me and Pete agreed not to tell you."

I blink. That must be why Pete didn't want to get back together with me last year. He felt guilty too.

"I always thought that you and Pete should be together, so I just wanted to forget about it," Carmen continues. Then she lets out a sigh. "I just thought I'd never get you back if you knew."

There's a look in her eyes I've never seen before but I'm so mad at her, I don't care what it is and turn away. How am I ever supposed to forgive her for what she has done? She's apologizing a year too late.

I open the door and slide in. Before I can shut the door, she comes up next to me.

"It's the Catskills."

I look up at her pleading eyes.

"What?"

"The clue on your paper heart. It's your Catskills house— I've been thinking about it all week."

I nod but can't bring myself to thank her now. Maybe not ever.

I shut the car door and start the engine. I'm not thinking about the fact that I haven't been able to drive for a year, or that each time I've tried I feel like I'm back in the hospital again, gasping for air. All I know is I need to get away, so that's what I do, not even looking at Carmen in the rearview mirror.

~

They say driving is like riding a bike. I never believed it until I was behind the wheel, driving by muscle memory.

Before I know it, I'm parked outside the library on another Friday night.

I strap my heels back on before getting out of the car. When I do, Andy sees me through the window. In seconds he rushes outside and soon his hands are on my face as he looks at the car, then back at me.

"Is everything okay? Did you drive here yourself? Why did you leave the dance?"

I hug him, and as I bury my face in his chest, I can feel his heart racing. But the smell of his cologne calms me.

"I'm fine," I say. "Well, sort of. Can I tell you in the car? We have a long trip ahead of us."

"Trip?" he asks, pulling back to see my face.

I nod. "I need to find my last paper heart."

"Tonight? What about your dance?"

"I can't wait any longer," I say.

This time Andy nods before wrapping his arms around me, his heart still beating fast.

Chapter 22

I'VE NEVER GONE TO MY FAMILY'S MOUNTAIN HOUSE WITH A boy before.

We mainly go in the winter as a family. My parents, Ashley, and I like to go skiing. I've always preferred the time we spend together post skiing—sitting by the fire with hot chocolate in hand or relaxing in the hot tub outside. In the summers we make use of our second home too. There's plenty of hiking around the Catskills. Ashley and I have gone to a few concerts at Woodstock. Two summers ago, I was able to invite my friends. Carmen, Jess, and I wore matching jean shorts and neon T-shirts that had Sunshine & Song lyrics printed on them. There's a framed picture in my bedroom from the concert where Carmen's on top of my shoulders. But I push this thought out of my head. I can't even think about her right now.

Once she's no longer in sight, I open the paper heart she

had stolen from me. It says, *The key to second chances is where your heart is.* She was right about the Catskills, but what she didn't know about was the bronze key I've kept on my lanyard. I had a feeling "the key" meant I was finally going to figure out what it opened.

I'm quiet for the majority of the car ride. Andy volunteers to drive but I insist on being the one behind the wheel. For some reason, it feels like this is something that I have to do.

So I drive for an hour and a half to the mountain house, trying to think about anything besides my traitor best friends. Each one of them calls. Every time the phone rings, the music from my phone stops playing and my ringtone blasts into the car. My phone's on the console so I can follow the GPS as I'm driving. The fourth call is from Katie. As the phone rings, I ignore it like I've ignored the others, but I can feel Andy staring at me.

"Are you going to get that?" he asks.

"No."

"So are you going to tell me what happened? Is this trip because my spontaneity is rubbing off on you, or does this spur-of-the-moment getaway have something to do with"—he pauses, reading the name on my phone—"Katie?"

"Both," I answer honestly, keeping my eyes on the road. "And I'll tell you. Just not tonight."

"Okay, I can wait for the drama. Until then I'll pretend you just wanted to whisk me away instead of having other boys asking you to dance all night."

"Sounding jealous over there. But for your information, no boys asked me to dance."

"Maybe because you left after ten minutes. But have you seen yourself tonight? I meant what I said. You look beautiful."

"Oh, in this old thing?" I laugh. I'm still in my dress, while Andy's in regular pants and a T-shirt. "Well, I'll be changing into my bathing suit once we get there."

"Um. Ella. I know you're having a crisis of some sort with your friends, but you do realize it's the dead of winter."

I laugh. "There's a hot tub."

"Hot tub!" he yells. "I can get used to this new and spontaneous Ella."

"Me too," I say as my cheeks turn warm, and not just from the heat blasting.

~

When we get to the house, the last thing I'm thinking about is the next paper heart. It's ironic, considering that's all I've been thinking about for the last few weeks. That's why I'm here to begin with.

But being alone with Andy—really alone—has made me focus solely on him. Maybe it's because the second we park in the driveway Andy hops out of the car and opens my door for me. Before he walks me to the house, he twirls me once under the moon and whispers in my ear that it's because I deserve at least one spin tonight when I look this good. Then he dips me like he did for our first kiss. When he does, all the tension built up from the car ride releases. It's like he sucks all the negative out of me. Here I am at my favorite place with my favorite person, and the funny part is that I didn't plan this—but here we are.

Andy takes my hand and we walk to the door. This feeling of safety mixed with excitement bursts inside me. It makes me walk faster, and soon I'm at the door, trying to let us in. I fiddle with my keys, thumbing the mystery bronze key, before finding one to the house.

"We made it." I exhale as we walk inside. I still can't believe we're here or that I'm the one who drove us here after all those months of not driving.

"We did. So tell me the plan," Andy says, spinning me again toward the living room.

"No plan," I say, smiling. "My dad keeps wood in the garage. If you know how to make a fire, that would be pretty nice right about now."

"As a matter of fact, I do," he says. "Fire and hot chocolate like you and your fam do?"

"You remember that?" I ask. I know I told him about my family vacations on our ride to NYC, but hearing him repeat it now is surprising in a good way.

"I remember everything you tell me," he says, rubbing my shoulders.

"Everything?" I ask.

"Mm-hmm. Like when you told me there was a hot tub that we can take advantage of."

"Oooh, hot tub, then fire and hot chocolate?"

He smiles. "Sounds like you're trying to plan now."

I frown. He's right.

"Hey," he says, kissing my forehead. "You know, I like that about you. And hot tub then fire sounds amazing. Let's do it."

"Really?"

He spins me again. "As much as I'm going to hate you changing out of this dress. Yes."

We kiss again until I can feel we're both smiling. "Go change," he whispers. I nod and head to my room. My bathing suit drawer is a mess, and it takes me longer to find a matching top and bottom than I expected. It's only when I try on my favorite black bikini that I feel self-conscious. I stand in front of the mirror, looking at the scar that runs along my chest from the accident. Normally I'm able to hide it, but there's no hiding it in this suit.

It's dark outside; he won't even be able to see it, I urge myself. But it only helps a little. I find a robe in my closet that I can wear until the last possible second.

As I make my way to the hot tub, I can hear the water rushing. Andy must have started to warm it up.

I move over to the window. Peering out, I can see that Andy's already inside. The hot tub is lit up, and I suddenly want to turn back around and say I changed my mind. But almost like he knows what I'm thinking he looks up and spots me. There's suddenly a huge smile on his face, and he waves me over. I take a deep breath. It's now or never.

I make my way to the sliding glass door. Opening it, I feel a burst of cold air. I run quickly to the hot tub. I'm barefoot, so my toes are cold as they hit the cement pathway my dad put in years ago.

When I reach the hot tub, I know that the faster I take my robe off, the faster I can get into the warm water, but I hesitate, looking at Andy. His hair is wet from going under. There's a small drop of water on his lips that I have the urge to kiss away, but it slides off when he talks.

"Are you coming in?" he asks, watching me hesitate.

"Yes," I say, but my body stays frozen where I'm standing. Maybe I can ask him to turn around. Then once I'm in the water, I can stay low so my scar is beneath the bubbles.

"What're you doing? I can't kiss you from all the way over here," he teases.

I sway awkwardly in my robe. It's not that I don't want to go in and kiss him. I do. I just wish with everything in me that I could go back to the days where I could put on a bathing suit feeling as confident as I did in the dress I wore tonight. But as I'm thinking this, Andy moves over to the edge of the hot tub to be closer to me.

"Is something wrong?" he asks.

"I . . . I have a scar," I confess. "From the accident. The second I go in there you're . . . you're going to see it."

His eyebrows furrow. "And you think I'll care? Is that really what you think of me?"

"No, not just you. Everybod—"

"I'm not everybody. I'm telling you that *nothing* is going to change the way I feel about you."

He reaches out his hand. His eyes are staring straight into mine—unflinching—and the way he's looking at me now makes me believe him.

Slowly, I untie the sash around my waist. Andy's eyes remain on mine. When the robe drops to the ground, he smiles his warm Andy smile. I quickly grab his hand and he pulls me toward him. I walk up the steps and then slide into the hot tub beside him. My body goes from freezing to warm in an instant.

Still holding my hand, Andy pulls me closer to him so that we're completely facing each other. The moonlight dances on his face.

He pulls our hands out of the water and brings the back of mine to his lips. He kisses it and then slowly starts kissing up my arm and up to my collarbone. My heart starts beating faster with his face so close to my scar, but when he kisses the spot right along my clavicle, I feel like I'm melting right here in this hot tub.

Soon he is at my lips, and when I kiss him back, I do so more passionately than I've ever kissed anyone. His hands move to my face and he holds me closer. I never want this kiss to end.

When eventually we pull away, he looks at me and brushes a piece of wet hair out of my face. "I love you, Ella Fitzpatrick."

At first, I'm not sure I hear him correctly over the bubbles around us but the look on his face tells me everything I need to know. He looks at me like I've always wanted to be looked at. He sees all of me.

I wrap my arms around his neck.

"I love you too."

With those words he finds my chin with his hand and lifts my mouth up to his mouth. He kisses me gently—so gently that it feels like my lips are fully absorbed into his.

Seconds turn to minutes. When we finally break for air, I don't know how long we've been in here, only that our hands have become pruned from being underwater.

We decide to head inside, sprinting as fast as we can to the house, my robe in hand. Still not tired of kissing him, I lead him to the shower. In between kisses we rinse each other off in our bathing suits, my breath speeding up as Andy's hands touch my skin.

After the shower we change back into our clothes and I make hot chocolate in the kitchen while Andy starts a fire in the living room.

Once we're both done, we sit together on the couch, sharing a blanket. Little pops come from the crackling fire. I rest my head on Andy's chest and he strokes my hair with his free hand. It's so soothing that I completely forget about everything that's happened in the past couple of weeks. All I can think about is that I meant what I said outside—I love this boy. It happened so quickly but it feels right—like everything that has happened so far was important because it led me to him.

There's nowhere else I'd rather be right now, I think. It's the last thought I have before I fall asleep, the fire crackling in the background.

Chapter 23

WHEN I WAKE UP IN MY BED, I KNOW ANDY MUST HAVE CAR-ried me here the night before.

I half expect him to be lying there with me, but when my arm reaches for him there's nothing but pillows.

I crack open my eyes. There on my nightstand is a piece of paper. It's folded in two so that it stands like a tent. The side facing me has my name written on it with a heart. I reach out and grab the note.

> *Ella,*
>
> *This isn't a paper heart but a promise that I'm going to come back with the best diner to-go food you've ever had.*
>
> *I love you,*
> *Andy*

I can't help but smile at how thoughtful Andy is. I put the letter carefully back on the nightstand—I'll definitely be keeping this for my secret hiding place. As I do, I realize that Andy has put my phone next to me as well, charging in the outlet by my bed. It's another thoughtful gesture, but I immediately feel a moment of dread seeing my phone as reality sets in. All of the memories from the school dance are coming back without Andy here to distract me.

I reluctantly grab my phone and see a bunch more missed calls and texts.

I scan through to the text from my sister.

Told Mom and Dad that you're at Katie's. Please tell me you're safe.

Ella . . .

I feel a surge of guilt and immediately text her that I'm fine. Then I add more.

In fact, I'm more than fine. SO much to tell you later. ILY.

I don't want to read any of the texts from my friends, especially from Carmen, but I don't have to click on her message to see what it says.

Andy isn't who he says he is. I'm trying to protect you.

I roll my eyes. Really? Now, after everything she said to me last night, she's going to try to say that about Andy? I'm so heated that I put my phone down. She has some nerve.

But it's my anger at her that reminds me of why I'm really here in the first place. Not for a romantic getaway with Andy—but to find the last paper heart. If I know one thing about planning, it's that you always save the best for last.

I begin roaming the house, searching for anything that can be opened with a key. If I'd been focused on the paper hearts yesterday, I would've been alarmed when I entered the house and there was nothing screaming out at me that said *open me.*

I really hope I didn't read the last paper heart wrong.

I shake my head. It has to mean here.

Moving quickly from room to room, I try everything that has a keyhole with my lanyard in hand. The first room I try is my parents', since I'm pretty convinced it has been my mom sending me these paper hearts.

There's a lockbox in the closet where emergency cash is stored. I only know this because it's also where my mom keeps her wedding rings when we go out on the ski slopes.

But as I try to put my key into the opening, it doesn't fit.

I keep trying to jam it in, growing more frustrated each time, until I admit defeat. What else could have a key in this room? I check the rest of the closet and there's nothing but snow boots and jackets. I move to the drawers on the other end of the room and sift through leggings and sweaters, to find absolutely nothing.

Where else would my mom keep something? Maybe the kitchen. She keeps her recipes in a little box next to the stove. I've seen it hundreds of times, but I don't recall a lock. I make my way to see it. There's a fake lock on the side of it that dangles like a charm. I search the rest of the cabinets and then the pantry. Nothing.

I let out a deep sigh. Maybe Carmen wasn't even right about the clue, like she wasn't right about anything this past year.

I go back to the living room, where I fell asleep in Andy's arms last night. Maybe I was too distracted to see something? I scan the shelf above the fireplace that we stream with a garland around the holidays. Now there are only our family photos. I check behind each frame and find nothing but dust.

Come on, Mom, I think, because I'm in the completely wrong place . . . unless the last paper heart is in Ashley's room. . . .

I run back upstairs to Ashley's room, which is adjacent to mine. Like at home, our rooms are complete opposites. Instead of keeping a calendar on her desk, she uses it as another space for a pile of clothes. Posters of her favorite bands cover every inch of the walls. Her bed is made, but only because my mom must have done it for her.

But then there—I see it. Square in the middle of her bed is a watercolored box with gold latches. It's vintage looking, in the shape of an old suitcase.

No, it can't be, I think.

I move swiftly toward the bed and bring the key to the box. My chest tightens as the key goes into the hole seamlessly. Then I turn it. With a soft *click,* the box opens.

There's a paper heart on top. My last letter.

Ashley? I think in amazement. *Ashley has been writing me these paper hearts?*

I feel my eyes start to well up. All this time I thought she was too cool for school to write me one paper heart, let alone eleven. What made her do it?

I was about to find out.

But as soon as I remove the last paper heart, my eyes move quickly to the Polaroid photo behind it. I recognize the setting immediately. Belvedere Castle. My eyes blink rapidly at the people in the center of the photo.

It's me, standing with Andy.

I reach into the box and flip over the photo.

Me and Drew 2/8

Drew? Who is Drew? This is Andy. My Andy. The Andy I fell in love with, who I met at the library . . . but no. This photo was clearly taken before then. We knew each other before the accident? I'm instantly hit with a wave of sickness. First my friends, now Andy. I don't know who to trust or believe anymore.

Suddenly, I remember the text from Carmen. *Andy isn't who he says he is. I'm trying to protect you.*

It's all I can think about now, and my head starts spinning as I burst into tears. Soon the tears turn to sobs. There's no point wiping them away at this point. They roll down my cheeks like waterfalls. I'm overwhelmed with emotion.

Suddenly, I hear a cheerful voice behind me.

"I'm back!"

I turn and there's Andy—or is it Drew—holding a bag with breakfast. He instantly spots the tears. His eyes dart from me to the picture I'm holding.

He takes a step toward me as I take a step back, my face still wet with tears.

"Let me explain."

Chapter 24

"EXPLAIN WHAT?!" I CRY. "THAT YOU *KNEW ME* BEFORE THE accident? Or that your name isn't even Andy? "

"Calm down, Ella," he says.

"Calm down! Don't tell me to calm down. I *trusted* you."

"You still can," he says, moving to sit on the bed. He looks at the spot next to him. "Can you please read the letter?"

"What can it possibly say that will make a difference?" I ask, still crying.

"Everything," he says.

Reluctantly, I move to sit next to him on the bed. I look at the box in my hands instead of him. I'm breathing fast as I move the key toward the latch again. When I open it this time, I pull out the paper heart. This one is not just a cutout, it's a long letter that I carefully unfold to read.

Dear Ella,

You must have guessed it by now, but yes, your secret admirer is me. Ashley. I've always been your admirer, really. You're the kind of sister that makes everything tough because I'm constantly trying to live up to your impossible standards. Maybe that's why sometimes I take it out on you.

But this isn't about me—this is about you. For a long time, I've been hoping, like you, that you'd fully recover and get your memory back. When it wasn't happening, I thought that I should take matters into my own hands and help guide you, like you have helped guide me throughout life as my big sister.

But I needed help. So I enlisted Drew. He told me everywhere the two of you went in the eleven weeks you forgot—the places where the two of you first fell in love. I can see it in your face now that you're falling in love again.

We steered you to the library so you could meet him again. He started working there with Sarah after the accident. I know it may be hard to believe, but Sarah was your closest friend during the time of the accident. In a way, he said seeing Sarah helped him stay close to you, even though you had completely forgotten who he was. Sarah too. He said his name was Andy in case it threw any of our plans off. His full name is Andrew. You actually met last year when his family moved to town. But please don't be mad at him. He was only trying to help you.

I think on some level the reason losing eleven weeks of your memory was so painful is because your heart didn't want you to forget. It knew you had a love out there waiting for you.

The night of the accident, you left the dance early because you and Drew were sneaking off to our mountain house for a romantic night. I only knew where you were going because I had to keep up your cover story, that you were sleeping at Carmen's. Mom and Dad weren't aware that you weren't speaking then. When I got the call from the hospital, I became racked with guilt over what I knew. But looking back, there's no way I would've tried to stop you. You were too in love. What kind of sister would I have been to get in the middle of that? And what kind of sister would I be to let you forget about it all?

I'll let Drew explain his side of the story. I've been

watching and I know you might have forgotten how to
follow your heart, but trust it now.

> *Love, Your Admirer,*
> *Ashley*

P.S. I've always known about your secret hiding spot.

I read the letter with my mouth open. Ashley has been trying to get me to remember *Andy*?

He clears his throat now. "Are you ready for my side of the story?"

I nod, still processing the letter.

"I know what you must be thinking. If we loved each other so much, why didn't I come find you?"

As I begin nervously folding the paper back into a heart, he continues. "But the thing is, I wasn't sure you'd even believe me. Love is something you feel. Not something you're told. I knew you fell in love with me once, so I was confident you would again. Then Ashley approached me with the idea of the paper hearts, and . . . I knew it was crazy, but I would do crazier things to get you back. Do you . . . do you remember anything . . . anything at all?"

He moves his hands over to mine. I flinch as our skin touches but he keeps his hand on mine as my breathing gets louder.

Do I remember anything?

"The flower shop?" I ask, recalling my first paper heart that led me to Clover and Gold.

"That's where we first met. You were ordering flowers for the Valentine's Day Dance. I was in the store getting flowers for my mom. When I saw you, I thought this is a girl who knows what she wants. I bought you a rose on the spot and got your number."

"I kept that rose," I say. He nods.

"The bridge?" I ask next. "Was that our first date?"

His eyes light up and he nods again.

"Then ice-skating?" I ask.

He smiles. "You're getting the idea."

"What about the spa?"

He laughs. "That's the only one we didn't do together. Ashley thought it would help you remember the dance."

"It didn't," I say bluntly.

He frowns. "I know. We also thought you were going to invite either her or me to the chocolate-making class. You threw us for a loop on that one."

Watching my eyes move back toward the Polaroid of us at Belvedere Castle, he grabs it. "And this," he adds, "is the day we first said 'I love you.'"

I look at the photo in front of me, remembering the one in my secret spot. I look *so* happy.

"Did we say I love you before this picture was taken?"

He shakes his head. "No, it was at the Whispering Gallery."

My heart drops. *This is romantic,* I tell myself. *He was trying to re-create your dates.*

But then why wasn't I happy? Maybe because I don't remember saying I love you to Andy at the Whispering Gallery. I remember saying it last night.

"It was all planned," I say now. There's a sadness in my voice.

"I thought you were going to be happy," he said. He lowers his head. "All this time, I wanted you to remember, but above all I just wanted you to be happy like we were last night."

"But it's a lie," I say now. "I fell in love with someone pretending they've never known me."

"I wasn't pretending to be me," he says. "That part was real. The love we share *is* real."

I turn away. "How am I supposed to believe that now?"

"Because you love me. You do, right?"

I look at him. When I don't respond right away, his eyes get wide and he bites his lip. It's something he's never done before in front of me—or at least not that I can remember. What else did I not remember?

"I know you're scared, El," he says. "But we can get through this together. If you don't remem—"

"Of course I'm never going to remember us again," I say now. It suddenly feels like all the hope I've had breaks in my mind. All this time I really thought I was going to regain my memory with these paper hearts. As my words are released, it feels like a giant weight has been lifted off me. "I might not ever remember how we first met."

My voice cracks at that last part. Is that why I'm so upset right now? I've dreamed forever of how I was going to meet the love of my life, keeping mementos to remember everything. But with Andy, I can't recall a thing. I begin sifting through the box again. There are more pictures of me and Andy. One of me in the passenger seat of his car.

"What about my friends?" I ask. "Did you know them too?"

He sighs. "You had a falling-out with them around the time we started dating. You were outgrowing them. They didn't like you hanging out with Sarah . . . or me," he admits. "Carmen didn't know what you saw in me and hated that you broke up with Pete for me."

Slowly, all the pieces begin sliding into place, but I don't remember. I have all the pieces, but I don't remember those eleven weeks. It feels like watching a movie with someone else playing me.

"I'm . . . I'm the girl who hurt you . . . ," I trail off.

"Well, yes, but it wasn't your fault. You didn't ask to forget me."

True, but I still did.

Andy studies my face. "What're you thinking?" he says.

I look at him, debating if I'm going to tell him. It's the one thing I won't be able to take back, but it's what is best.

"I know you've given me a year, but I need more time."

Chapter 25

SPRING

"WE COULD SELL CARNATIONS," TOMMY SUGGESTS. HE'S the freshman who gave me my paper hearts in the cafeteria back in February. I learned his name when I rejoined student government in March.

"We can be more original than carnations," Sarah says, shaking her head. The two braided buns on the sides of her head move back and forth.

"But how?" Brian asks. "The only other thing on our fund-raising list for the Spring Fling is a kissing booth, which will *never* get approved by Principal Wheeler.

Sarah looks at me, because we spent the weekend brainstorming.

"Sarah and I have been thinking," I start. "It's a little more complicated than hearts, but if we do a flower design, we can hold the same fund-raiser we have for the paper hearts." Sarah reaches into the bag she bought at the Brooklyn Flea last weekend when we went on a day trip together. She pulls out two paper flowers we made as examples on the train ride back. "Voilà!" she says, holding them up for everyone to see. We used cool patterned pink paper and cut it in the shapes of lilies.

"Oooh, let me see!" a girl named Patrice says, grabbing one. Sarah passes the other to another girl, Lauren, next to her.

"How's copying ourselves original?" Tommy argues.

"It's totally different," Sarah says. "Besides, everyone needs a little pick-me-up for spring. What better way to spread cheer than with paper flowers?"

As the others in the group nod, the vote becomes unanimous. We'll be doing paper flowers to raise money for Spring Fling. Sarah squeezes my hand in excitement.

My first idea back on the planning committee is approved.

⁓

After the meeting, Sarah and I drive to Smoothie King to celebrate. Ashley comes too. I order a strawberry-and-pineapple one, and once we all have our drinks, we find a table outside.

"To the Idea Queen," Sarah says as she raises her smoothie. Ashley raises hers too.

"You guys don't have—" I start.

"Come on!" Ashley interrupts. "We're just waiting on you."

I reluctantly raise my smoothie and we toast.

"Thank you both," I say before taking a sip. "For celebrating with me . . . and, well, for everything."

A lot of things changed after I found my last paper heart.

I haven't spoken to Carmen since the night of the Valentine's Day Dance. I'm not saying there won't be a day when I forgive her. But if I let her back in now, I won't forgive myself.

I haven't spoken to Jess either, but Katie has been reaching out a lot lately, apologizing. She asked if we could meet up at Pink Drinks to talk. I said I'd love to talk but that we should try something different for a change. The plan is still in the works, but we're getting together next week.

In the meantime, I rejoined student government and became friends with Sarah again, which is amazing because we're both starting school at Columbia in the fall. We haven't been friends again for very long, but it feels like I've known her for ages. From everything I've learned over the past year, I can say one thing: people change like the weather, but you have to find the friends that brighten your day like a ray of sunshine and the ones that will be by your side in a storm.

Oh, and those social media passwords I could never figure out—I tried Andrew's birthday and was finally able to log in to my accounts. Life is funny like that. I have also created a new page just for my book quote calligraphy, which has been exploding.

"You don't need to thank me *again*," Ashley says now. "I think a hundred and one times is enough. Although you could . . . ," she says, looking at Sarah. "Never mind."

"Could what?" I demand. "Say it."

She bites her lip. "I'm just wondering when you're going to thank Drew. He was part of it too, you know."

My cheeks burn at his name. Maybe because she called him Drew instead of Andy. Plus, he's all I've been thinking about these past couple of weeks, no matter how hard I've tried to forget him. The irony is not lost on me.

"I think you should at least talk to him. You said it yourself on the train ride this weekend that you miss him."

I glare at her. "Whose side are you on?"

"We just want you to be happy," Ashley says. "And you were so happy with Andrew. What's holding you back?"

"He tried to re-create our love story. I get how that's romantic, but it's just not . . ." I trail off.

"Not what you wanted your love story to be?" Sarah finishes.

I nod. "I know it's silly. And after all that, I can't imagine Andy . . . I mean Andrew. I can't imagine him wanting to be with a girl who turned down a romantic gesture like that. Talk about ungrateful. All this time I've known him, I thought he was slightly jaded about love because of some old girlfriend, and that ended up being me. I don't want to mess up more than I already have," I say, looking down at my smoothie.

"Why can't you just say all that?" Sarah says, like it's easy.

"Oh yeah, like when you didn't want to tell me we were actually friends because Carmen said she'd tell me and everyone else you were crazy?"

"That's different," she says. "I didn't want to confuse you during an already confusing time. And I didn't tell you that so you could use it against me, you jerk."

"We're just surprised that you don't have a plan, is all," Ashley starts. "I mean, think about everything I did for you. The spying on you to find out where you were. The organization of the paper hearts, plotting when to deliver each one. Pretending to be you is hard."

"Who said I don't have a plan?" I say, pulling a paper heart out of my bag.

"What heart is that?" Ashley asks.

I shake my head. "It's not one of the hearts you gave me. It's a new one I wrote to Andrew. I just haven't figured out what to do with it."

Sarah and Ashley's eyes widen. "Give it to him!" they yell in unison.

"I can't just give it to him. I haven't seen him in weeks. . . ."

"So? He waited for you for *a year*," Sarah says. "Don't you get this is a love story meant to happen?"

"It's true," Ashley says. "Why do you think I broke up with Steve? You gave me hope for a better love story."

I look at both my best friend and my sister pleading in front of me.

"Come on," Ashley says. "You were the one who started this paper hearts thing for a reason—so people could tell one another how they really feel. This is your chance."

"When should I do it?"

"Now!" they scream again in unison.

"But really," Sarah says. "And I happen to know he's working."

I take a deep breath before nodding. They're right—this is something I need to do, not just for *us* but for me.

If I'm being honest with myself, he's the real reason I felt so lost this year. Now I know why—he borrowed my heart like a library book, but he never really gave it back.

~

My palms are sweating as I make my way up the steps of the library to where we first met.

Or at least where *I* remember meeting Andrew.

When I walk inside, he's sitting at the front desk, reading a book. I sigh. His hair is a little messy like the last time I saw him.

He looks up and his mouth drops. I quickly walk over to him.

"Hey," I say when I reach the desk.

"Hey," he says back. All my nerves disappear as his dimple appears.

"I don't mean to bother you at work," I say. "But I have something I wrote. Something I need to read to you. Is that okay?"

He looks around. "Only if you use your library voice."

I smile. "I can do that."

I reach into my purse and remove the paper heart I've been carrying around with me for a couple of weeks. The creases in the paper are deep from how many times I've opened the letter and then refolded it. The words I'm about to read are practically memorized.

"'All my life I dreamed about how I'd meet my person. Maybe at a concert or across the room. I'd read stories and hope that my love story would be like a fairy tale. It sounds cliché but it's true,'" I say. I look up from my paper and see Andrew smiling. My hands are shaky as I clutch the letter, but his smile keeps me going.

"'But it's not the beginning of a story that matters. It's how you end it. If my accident taught me anything, it's that life isn't picture-perfect. You don't get to plan what life throws at you. You can't plan love. But you can plan to do what makes you happy.'" I look up with a small tear threatening to escape my eye. There's no need to read the letter now. The rest is straight from the heart.

"I believe in love letters and sweet memories that you can

keep forever in the back of your mind. I believe in the power of first love and second chances. I believe in looking up at the stars and the twinkle in your eyes. I still believe that once in your life you meet someone that changes everything. I may not remember how I met you, but I remember how you made me feel—and that's why I'm here. To tell you that I was wrong. We both were. You re-creating our love story was the most romantic thing anyone has ever done for me, but it's not our love story anymore."

I move closer to him. "I . . . I want to start a new love story with you."

In one quick swoop he reaches across the desk and takes my face in his hands. "It would be my privilege to go on another love mystery adventure with you," he says. My heart has never beat faster.

Then we kiss. We kiss as people start clapping at the tables nearby. We kiss as he holds my face tighter. We kiss as I feel him smile with my lips.

Once we finally let go, I hand him the paper heart I read him.

"I get to keep it? Why, thank you," Andrew says, grinning.

"Yeah, but you have to read the clue at the bottom."

"Clue?" He raises an eyebrow.

"Yeah, since I don't remember our first real date and our second first date doesn't count, I'm declaring today our first real date. Well, dates, really. There are eleven spots total—get ready for the best day ever."

"Oh yeah? Well, where are we going first?" he asks, while reading the clue underneath my message. Andrew smiles. "Okay, but you better have gone easy on me...."

"Never," I answer. Then I lean over and kiss him again, and it truly feels like we're starting our new love story. And this time, I know I'm going to remember every detail.

Acknowledgments

A special thanks to my editor extraordinaire, Wendy Loggia, who gave this book so much love, and to my brilliant designer, Casey Moses, whose hand-lettering would make Ella proud. I'd also like to give eleven paper hearts to Bonnie Cutler, Lili Feinberg, Colleen Fellingham, Erica Henegen, Beverly Horowitz, Alison Impey, Jenn Inzetta, Victoria Rodriquez, Alison Romig, Tamar Schwartz, and Elizabeth Ward for their hard work making this book possible. Most of all, thank you to my friends, family, and real-life adventure partners for the inspiration.

Don't miss another swoon-worthy
read from Underlined!

Chapter One

Growing up in New York City is a crash course in the art of self-defense. I don't mean learning martial arts or the proper way to use a stun gun or anything like that. I mean, quickly and accurately assessing people and situations for potential disasters so you can avoid them before they happen.

That discounted MetroCard someone's trying to sell you on the street? It's a scam.

That guy sitting in the corner of the subway car, making kissy noises and hissing in your direction? Don't make eye contact.

That one lonely cockroach you saw zooming across your kitchen counter the other day? It's *never* one lonely cockroach. Trust me when I say there's a million more where that came from. Have your parents call the landlord, pronto.

Basically, if you want to survive (and keep your apartment vermin-free), you need to know trouble when you see it.

And I know trouble when I see it.

This morning, trouble takes the form of Jason Eisler, strolling into American History with a goofy grin and an easy stride.

On the surface, there's nothing concerning going on here. Just a teenage boy rolling into class, hands in the pockets of his hoodie, backpack bouncing with each step.

But I know Jason too well not to be concerned. There's a certain subtle glimmer he gets in his chocolate-brown eyes when he's up to no good. The first time I remember seeing it, we were in second grade, and he'd somehow managed to sneak a lifelike rubber tarantula into our teacher's top desk drawer. When poor Ms. Chen opened it up, she went paler than Marshmallow Fluff, shrieking so loudly that one of the girls at table two started to cry. Five minutes later, the principal showed up in our classroom, his bushy eyebrows furrowed with disdain as Ms. Chen explained what happened. Jason wasn't fazed, though. He just giggled, eyes glimmering, as he followed the principal out the door.

In the intervening decade, Jason's pranks have become more sophisticated, more interesting, but that glimmer in his eyes is still the same. It dances a little now when he looks my way.

"What's up, Ashley?" he calls from the front of the room. People turn to check me out, but I slide farther down in my chair and glare at the scratched desktop. I want no part of whatever he's got planned.

The bell chimes to signal the start of the period, and five seconds later, Ms. Henley closes the classroom door. "Take your seats, please," she says. After everyone settles in, she projects a slideshow about the Cuban Missile Crisis onto the whiteboard. You'd think she'd go easy on us since it's the last day of school before two weeks of spring break, but that has never been Ms. Henley's style.

"Today we're going to discuss the role diplomacy played in . . ." Her voice trails off when the door squeaks open, and

I think I see a thin curl of smoke wafting from each of her nostrils. Ms. Henley *hates* latecomers. Her shoulders hunch toward her ears, and I can tell she's preparing to lay into this unfortunate soul with a tirade about time wasting and personal responsibility. But when she sees who it is, her shoulders relax again.

It's Walker Beech, the opposite of trouble.

He looks appropriately contrite. "Sorry I'm late, Ms. Henley."

"It's okay, Walker." She waves away his apology with a casual smile. "We were just getting started."

Only Walker Beech could elicit such a warmhearted response from the iciest teacher at Edward R. Murrow High School.

As Walker slips inside and gently closes the door behind him, I try not to stare. It's no use, though. His body's like a magnet dragging my attention away from Ms. Henley, who's now gesturing toward a map of Cuba. She's droning on about the Bay of Pigs, but all I can focus on is Walker's hair, the way his thick brown curls defy gravity. I wonder if he spends a lot of time getting them so flawlessly tousled or if it's a natural phenomenon. Probably the latter.

At least I'm not the only one distracted by his magnificence. From my vantage point in the middle of the classroom, I can see at least three other people—Chelsea, Yaritza, Marcus— watching his every move. Their heads turn in unison, tracking him as he walks down the fourth row of desks, headed for the empty seat directly to my left.

Omigod.

He's sitting next to me.

In one motion, I sit up straight and tuck my hair behind my ears, smoothing any flyaways. Not that he's looking at me or anything. As he passes me, I get a whiff of his cologne. It smells like one of those clove-scented oranges Mom sets around the table at Christmastime.

The moment he slides into his chair, he's already engrossed in the lesson, notebook open to a blank sheet of paper, pen uncapped, ready to write. He squints his hazel eyes at the whiteboard, clearly fascinated by Ms. Henley's discussion of geopolitical strife at the height of the Cold War.

So dreamy. So mysterious.

That's the thing about Walker Beech—the thing that makes him the opposite of trouble. He's always attentive in class, always completely respectful. I didn't know him in second grade, but I'm certain he never hid a rubber tarantula in his teacher's top desk drawer.

Okay! Enough obsessing over Walker Beech.

As I'm finally tuning in to Ms. Henley's monotonous speech, I'm distracted yet again. This time by Jason, who's fidgeting in his chair, shifting awkwardly with his arms folded across his chest. I'm sure he's uncomfortable sitting in the front row, right under Ms. Henley's nose, but it's not like he has a choice in the matter. Those fart noises he made on the first day of the semester earned him the distinct honor of being the only person in class with an assigned seat.

No one else seems clued in to Jason's restlessness, but that's not a surprise. Like I said, I know him really well.

And I know when he's hiding something.

Right now, that something appears to be shiny and cylindrical and candy-apple red, because I see the end of it slipping out the bottom of his hoodie. He shifts again and it disappears. Behind him, Dmitry Yablokov props his phone up on his desk, angled beside his binder so Ms. Henley can't see it—if she did, it would be locked in her file cabinet in two seconds flat. When he sets the video and slides his thumb to the record button, alarm bells go off in my head.

Trouble.

Sure enough, Jason gets to his feet.

"Sit down, Mr. Eisler." Ms. Henley's voice is sharp but exasperated. Predictably, Jason acts as if he hasn't heard her.

He turns to face the class, one hand waving in the air, the other one reaching behind his back, presumably keeping that shiny, cylindrical, candy-apple-red thing from falling out beneath his hoodie. A few giggles echo around the room. Several people suck their teeth.

"Guess what, everybody?" he yells. "It's my birthday!"

It isn't his birthday. Today is March 25, and he turns seventeen on April 10. But this bald-faced lie isn't the biggest problem at hand.

Ms. Henley knows it, because she sighs and pushes her glasses up onto her head. When she pinches the bridge of her nose, her eyes close just long enough to miss the moment when Jason whips out the cylinder. It's about two feet long, with the words PARTY POPPER emblazoned on the side.

A confetti cannon.

This should be fun.

"Let's have a party!" he yells.

A split second later, there's a deafening crack. Ms. Henley shrieks, sounding exactly like Ms. Chen did in the second grade. The classroom is showered with colorful tissue paper. It flits through the air, glittering in the fluorescent overhead lights, pink and blue and silver and gold. It lands in our hair, on our clothes, all over our desks and the floor. Our boring social studies lesson has been transformed into the grand finale of a Taylor Swift concert.

It's actually kind of magical. I can't help smiling.

Everyone else is smiling, too, even the people who were sucking their teeth ten seconds ago. Chatter and laughter erupt. A few daredevils reach for their phones, but Ms. Henley immediately puts the kibosh on that.

"Don't even think about taking pictures or I'll lock up your phones until you return from spring break!"

Dmitry's phone is already out of sight. He's all innocence and wonder now, playfully tossing handfuls of confetti at Rachel Gibbons, as if he hadn't been the designated camera-man for this spectacle.

I wonder how Jason convinced him to do it. Probably cash. All those hours Jason spends stocking shelves with me at the Shop Rite, only to throw it away making these videos.

See, last year Jason decided to broaden his audience and expand his reach from our overstuffed Brooklyn high school to the entire world—or, at least, to anyone with internet access. He has dreams of going viral.

Lately, these videos have taken over his life. He doesn't participate in a single legitimate extracurricular activity—you know, something he can list on his college applications. Me? I'm a peer math tutor, a Mathlete, and a member of the Coding Club. And while I do enjoy these extracurriculars, I also chose them very deliberately, to show prospective universities how serious I am about pursuing a STEM degree. They're strategic moves.

Jason never does anything strategically.

Case in point: the current debacle in our confetti-covered classroom.

"Unacceptable!" Ms. Henley's face is as red as the now-empty cardboard tube dangling from Jason's right hand. "You'll be lucky if you don't get expelled!"

"For a few scraps of tissue paper?"

Her face grows redder still. "In this day and age, Mr. Eisler, the sound of a firecracker is not to be taken lightly, particularly inside a school. The threat of violence is real, and it is no laughing matter!"

For the first time, his confidence wavers. I can tell because the glimmer is gone and his lips twitch the tiniest bit. Imperceptible to most; unmistakable to me.

"But I wasn't threatening anything," he says. "I was just—"

"To say nothing of the mess you've created in my classroom!"

She's breathing heavily now, the wheeze of her smoker's lungs audible from halfway across the suddenly silent room. Jason's lip twitches again, and I wonder if maybe he's feeling a twinge of regret.

I steal a glance at Walker, but he doesn't seem to care about the drama unfolding before our eyes. Instead, he's looking down at his lap, where his thumbs tap frantically against his phone screen.

It's a bold move to be texting in Henley's class. Then again, she's dealing with more pressing matters right now, and Walker's discreet. He may be breaking the rules, but it's a quiet, clever defiance.

Walker Beech is strategic.

"You know what?" Jason says. "You're right. I didn't realize there was gonna be so much confetti in this thing. Lemme run to the custodian's office real quick to grab a broom so I can clean it up."

Ms. Henley looks personally offended. "Oh no. You're going to the dean, immediately." She walks over to the wall-mounted landline beside the door and jabs at the keypad. "I'm calling him now so he knows to expect you."

As she grouses into the handset, Rachel Gibbons calls out, "Happy birthday, Jason!"

Just like that, the glimmer in his eyes is back.

Rachel knows it's not really his birthday. At least, she *should* know—she's his ex-girlfriend, after all. They dated for eight months, from the end of last school year until the beginning of January. I'm tempted to call her out on it, but then I realize she might be in on this prank. She's the whole reason he decided to start recording these videos in the first place.

Soon the whole class starts singing the birthday song. I don't want to seem like a wet blanket, so I mumble along. Then Ms. Henley slams the phone back on the wall and spins around. "Quiet down!" The singing ends abruptly. She points one stubby finger toward the door and glares at Jason. "Dean Ross is waiting for you, Mr. Eisler. I suggest you leave immediately."

"Will do." He slings the cardboard tube over his shoulder like a hobo stick and turns to leave. With his hand on the door-knob, he pauses and looks back at me, the glimmer dancing in his eyes.

"Out!" Ms. Henley shrieks, and he's gone.

If the prank itself was the finale of a Taylor Swift concert, then the present moment is fifteen minutes after the encore, when the lights are too bright and the floor is a mess and you're trapped in a bottleneck of hundreds of people trying to cram themselves through a few narrow stadium doors. The mundane reality of life is painful after such an extravagant show.

Maybe Ms. Henley feels the same way. Maybe the silver lining on this confetti cloud is a temporary reprieve from history class. With all the excitement—not to mention the mess—surely there's no way we could be expected to continue with this lesson.

"Don't think you're getting out of this lesson!" Ms. Henley sweeps a few stray pieces of tissue paper off her laptop and taps the trackpad. On the whiteboard, the map of Cuba is replaced with a bullet-pointed list of keywords beside a black-and-white photo of JFK. "I'll clean this all up after the period's over. Right now, it's back to work."

So much for a silver lining.

Everyone settles down so Ms. Henley can resume her lecture, but I'm too amped up to concentrate. There's a buzzing in my ears, almost like I'd actually been to a concert, and my brain feels fuzzy. Even if I was interested in the intricacies of the Cold War, I probably couldn't process a word coming out of Ms. Henley's mouth right now.

My eyes slide to Walker, who's back to being focused and disciplined. Notebook open, pen at the ready, phone nowhere to be seen. Ever the opposite of trouble.

Not for the first time, I wonder what his hair feels like. Is it soft and silky, or sticky with product? If I sank my fingers into those thick, brown curls, would they slide through easily or get tangled up in knots?

And I just now noticed: his hands are *impeccable.* Square palms. Strong knuckles. Clean, trim fingernails. He grips his ballpoint pen with purpose as it glides across his college-ruled paper. I can't see what he's writing, but I'm sure his notes are insightful interpretations of whatever Ms. Henley is blathering about.

Suddenly, his pen stops moving, which is weird because Ms. Henley's still talking. My gaze drifts upward from his hand to his face and oh god those hazel eyes are aimed right at me.

I've been caught staring.

This is a *disaster*.

My brain screams, *Look away, Ashley!* But I can't. The magnetic force of his body has pulled me in.

His brows knot together—confused, amused, who can tell?—and then the corners of his perfect mouth turn up. I'm not sure if he's laughing at me or with me, but I do know this is the first time he's ever looked at me. Like, *really* looked at me.

My breath comes fast and shallow, and when Walker drops his pen on his notebook, I stop breathing altogether. Because his impeccable hand is reaching across the aisle, and now it's in my hair, and it's possible I may pass out from lack of oxygen.

When he pulls his hand away, there's a slender scrap of pink paper pinched between his thumb and forefinger. He shows it to me with a smile, then lets it flutter to the floor.

Immediately, he resumes his note-taking, but I'm not even in the classroom anymore. I'm at the finale of a Taylor Swift concert.

No, scratch that. I'm in Times Square on New Year's Eve. The ball's just dropped and everyone's cheering and confetti is flying around like magic pixie dust.

Walker Beech touched me.

There's my silver lining.